INSIDE OUT IZZY

Mom talks with Izzy
About Energy, Experience and Thought

© Angela Mastwijk 2014
A Sunsureness Creation
Illustrations: Karin van Kempen
Edited by: Pamela Wilson

ISBN 978-1-291-98093-6

Chapters

CHAPTER 1

Who is Izzy?

Izzy is nine years old. She's in Primary 5 with Miss Marion. Izzy isn't tall, but she's not short either. Mom recently measured her at four and a half feet. Her shoe size is 2.5. Izzy has long, blonde hair. Her eyes are green. At school she's really good at reading and kind of bad at math. Izzy loves to draw. It's her favourite hobby.

Izzy lives in a small town, in a street with rather large houses. Every two houses share one roof. These are called semi-detached. They all have a garage and a garden. Behind the garden there's a forest with big, old trees. Izzy likes to play there. Her mother has an office in the garage. That's simply a room with a table and comfy chairs. Mom talks to people there all day and sometimes in the evenings too.

Mom has green eyes, just like Izzy. But her hair is dark and not that long. Mom isn't tall or short. Izzy's Dad is really tall though. He sometimes has to duck when walking through a door! Dad is light-haired. His eyes are blue. He has a small beard that doesn't tickle. Dad is in the computer business. He has his own company. About a dozen people work there. Dad has a fancy name for what he does, a name Izzy can never remember. But it's an easy job, she thinks. Because Dad is often home early.

Izzy has no brothers or sisters. She does have a dog and his name is Spike. At first he didn't have a name. Izzy called him 'Puppy'. One day Puppy was all wet because it was raining. His hair was all spiky. Dad said, "Puppy's got spikes!" Right then Izzy knew 'Spike' was her dog's new name.

Spike is big and brown. He looks like a labrador but he isn't. Spike has thick, plump legs but he can run quite fast with them. He's smart and soft and loves to cuddle. Izzy went to dog training with Spike and Dad. Now he listens very well. Spike, that is. And he has to, because he's the same weight as Izzy and he's much stronger than her. He could easily topple her over. Spike loves the forest, Izzy and chewy dog treats.

Izzy usually wears jeans and a t-shirt. She doesn't like skirts or dresses. Nina is her best friend. So ... now you know who Izzy is.

But ... wait a minute ... is that really true? Izzy's lying on her back on the trampoline in the back garden. She's wearing a thick jacket and a woollen hat. It's winter. Izzy's looking up at the clouds in the sky. She spots funny animals, monsters and people in the clouds. They very quickly change form all the time. Sometimes she's watching a cloud and she sees a pig. A minute later, the same cloud is a crocodile. Or a snail. Or an elephant. Or a giant with a weird nose.

Suddenly Izzy thinks, 'I change form all the time, too! Just like those clouds. But I don't think as fast. Who AM I really then, if everything about me changes all the time? Of course I have a name, Izzy. But it doesn't say anything about me. Besides, Dad sometimes calls me Izzybusy. For fun, just to tease me a bit. My Nan always calls me Isabella. That sounds very fancy. It's Nan's own name as well and I've been named after her. Nan is proud of that. I listen to all those names. But is it really who I am?'

Izzy continues her thinking. 'I'm nine now, but I'll turn ten in July. My age will always be changing. So it's not who I am. I'm still growing too. Very fast, according to Mom. I have no idea how tall I will become! Nan says she's shrinking again. 'She probably makes her baths too hot'. Izzy softly giggles at that thought. 'My shoe size changes as well.' Izzy hopes her feet will grow rapidly. She'd like to have new boots. Buying shoes is fun. Especially when she and Mom go and have a hot chocolate with whipped cream afterwards.

Izzy looks down at her body again. 'My hair is blonde, but I could colour it. Black maybe, with purple highlights. And I could put coloured lenses in my eyes! Brown would be nice, I guess. Everything about my body can change. So it's not who I am.'

'How about what I know?' Izzy thinks. 'And what I do? I learn something new every day in school. Perhaps I'll understand math much better one day. Perhaps not. Now I love to draw, but I might get other hobbies. What I know and what I do is not who I am either.'

Izzy ponders what else she knows about herself. 'My address!' she thinks. 'But where I live now can change. We might move. Not that I would want to because I like it here. Except for David, that is.' David is the boy who lives next door.

How about what she thinks and feels? 'Sometimes I feel sad. I can be angry once in a while. Most of the time I'm in a cheerful mood. I think. How I feel, changes all the time and what I think too. One day I think I have the funniest Dad in the world. The next day I think he's boring when he takes ages reading the newspaper. Sometimes I think about Grandad who died, but often I don't. I think all day long. Different things all the time! It's not who I am.'

Izzy sees a cloud that looks like an icecream cone. With a big heap of cream. 'Mmm, that looks yummy!' she thinks. Then it occurs to her, 'I used to hate lettuce when I was little. But now I like it. And I never drink milk but when I was a baby I did, every day. My tastes change too, I guess. It's not who I am.'

Izzy sees Spike in the kitchen. He's sniffing around near the counter top. 'Spike must be hungry,' she thinks. 'He's always hungry. Spike would eat all day if you let him. Funny dog. Izzy realizes she's Spike's boss. 'But Mom and Dad are his boss too. Spike will die one day. Hopefully not until he's very old. Then I'll still be here, but not as Spike's boss. So it's not who I am.'

'I'm Dad and Mom's child until I'm grown up. Then I'll still be their child, of course. Until they're gone. I'll be old myself by that time. I think. But I won't be somebody's child forever. It's the same with being someone's friend. Sometimes, when Nina and I have an argument, we're no longer friends. That usually doesn't last very long. But it does change. I'm a pupil as long as I'm in school. I hope not for too long, though. I'm David's next door neighbour, perhaps until we're grown ups. I'm the grandchild of two grandmothers and a grandfather. I'm the niece of two uncles and three aunts. They're Mom's three sisters. I'm Rose, Max, Simon and Laura's cousin. And however long it lasts, it can all change. It's not who I am.'

Spike walks into the garden. Izzy pats her hand on the trampoline. Spike immediately knows what she means. He's a smart dog - most of the time. He runs up and jumps onto the trampoline. Izzy flies into the air and laughs. When she comes down again, Spike wobbles on his legs. He quickly lies down. Izzy bounces around on her knees, so that

Spike goes up and down. He enjoys that. Spike licks Izzy's face with his huge tongue. Izzy buries her face in his thick, soft neck. She tickles Spike behind his ears. They lay there together for a while. Softly rocking on the trampoline.

Izzy continues to think. 'So, I'm not my name. I'm not my body, or my hobbies. I'm not the place where I live. Nor am I what I know or what I eat. I'm not my relationship to the people and animals around me. It's all a story about me. It changes all the time. What is it that remains unchanged then? Who am I?'

Izzy is looking for an answer, but can't find one. She shrugs. 'Oh well,' she thinks, 'I guess I don't know. That's fine with me.' She can feel, however, that there's more to the story. Something beyond the story. She's sure about that. She just hasn't got a name for it.

CHAPTER 2

The Sun is Always There

Izzy stares up into the sky for a while longer. Clouds are passing by. Then the sun shines on her face. 'That's it!' Izzy suddenly realises. 'I'm not like the changing clouds, but I'm like the sun! A light. But it's shining from the inside. Something like that.' The words now pop into her head effortlessly. 'A light in my body. Somewhere near my heart, I think. Perhaps it IS my heart! It has no name and no story. The light is always there. Just like the sun!'
Izzy is sure now. 'The sun is always there, too. Although you can't always see it. It's rather funny. All people know this. But they talk as if they DON'T know. They say, 'the sun isn't shining today' when the weather is bad. But that's not true. The sun is always there but is simply covered by clouds. And we say the sun comes up, but that isn't true either. The earth is just spinning around and then you see the sun again. In the evening the sun doesn't disappear. Our piece of the earth simply turns away from it. Could there be more things that work like that? In the world and in our lives? That we're thinking are true but aren't true at all?'

Izzy is still lying comfortably on her trampoline. She listens to the birds in the garden. The sparrows have found her peanuts. When it's freezing, Izzy and her Dad make long strings with nuts for them. They seem to be happy with it, judging by the noise they make. The sparrows are chittering loudly. Then Izzy gets an idea. It's a nice drawing she wants to make. She can already picture it in her mind. She sees a colourful bird on a branch. Izzy jumps up and quickly performs a back-flip. The move startles Spike a bit. He jumps off the trampoline and runs ahead of her. Izzy skips inside the house. She gets her pencils out and a piece of paper.

Izzy is still in the kitchen and drawing when Mom comes in. She's finished talking for today. Mom gives Izzy a hug. "How was your day, honey?" Mom wants to know. "Nice, I guess," Izzy says. The drawing has made her forget everything. The world around her and her day at school. Mom makes them a cup of tea. Then Izzy remembers her thinking about the clouds and the sun. She tells Mom what she has been wondering about. About who she is.

"That's funny," Mom says, "that's exactly what I talk about all day, with the people who come to see me." "Really?" Izzy is surprised. She can hardly believe it. Do those grown-ups still have no idea who they are? "Well who do you think you are?" Mom wants to know. "Well," Izzy says, "at first I could only come up with the things I was NOT!" "That's a good start," Mom smiles, "you're on the right track already!" Izzy hasn't got a clue what Mom is talking about It's a good thing that she doesn't know anything? "Huh?" she says, quite confused. "I'll try to explain something to you," Mom says. "tonight, before you go to sleep, all right? Instead of a bedtime story." "Sure," Izzy nods, "but if it's too boring we're going to read from my new book, okay?" Mom agrees. Then Izzy tells her what she has been thinking about the clouds and the sun. And about the light. "I don't need to tell you anything new," Mom smiles.

So Izzy's Mom talks to people all day, every day. Like a teacher, sort of. Izzy doesn't know what she talks about. What she does know, is that most people go home looking quite happy and relaxed. More happy and relaxed than when they came in. Izzy can see that because there's a door between the hallway and the garage. This way, Izzy can quickly go to her Mom when she wants to say or ask something. Izzy has learned she has to wait until the person Mom has been talking with, leaves. Then she runs through the door to give her Mom a kiss. Or to tell her that she's going to play at Nina's house. Or to ask whether she's allowed to take an ice cream from the freezer when it's really warm.

While Izzy's waiting, she can hear Mom talking quietly. Or the other person says something. Sometimes it's silent for a while. Or Mom and the person are laughing out loud. Nice conversations seem to be going on in there. Izzy can never hear what they're saying. But now Mom is going to tell her everything she teaches her clients. If it's not too boring, that is.

CHAPTER 3

Three Popsicles

That night at bedtime, Mom walks upstairs with Izzy. Izzy crawls under her duvet. Only her eyes and her hair peep out. Mom nestles herself in the big beanbag beside her bed. "Well," she begins. "I'm going to tell you something about three laws. The laws of life. It's about who you really are. You've already discovered something this afternoon. You called it a light. I think that's very smart. These laws also explain how life works. You've already seen that the sun is always present. But we talk about it as if it's not. We say the sun disappears and comes back, but it's the clouds that come and go. We say the sun comes up and goes down, but it's the other way around. Our earth is spinning. And it's the same with life. It's not how we think it is. It works in a different way than we're saying. In fact, it works exactly the other way around. "The other way around?" Izzy asks. "You mean upside down?"

There she goes. Izzy's hanging upside down from her bed. With her feet on the pillow and her long hair on the floor. "Well," Mom giggles, "perhaps I'll change that to inside out." "That's just gross," Izzy says. "If I would be turned inside out!" "Yuck ... I don't even want to think about it," Mom laughs.

"But I don't mean your body when I say 'inside out'. I'm talking about your experience. That's a difficult word maybe. Wait a minute." Mom closes her eyes and calmly waits until the right words come into her head.

"Let's put it this way. We think that the world is just out there. A lot of things are happening and we react to them. We have an opinion about them. The sun shines and we're happy. It rains and we're sad. Someone likes us and we're glad they do. Someone bullies us and we feel bad and hurt. Or we feel angry. "'Of course!" Izzy cries out. "Bullying is stupid, isn't it? You can't be happy when you're being bullied, can you? If someone bullies you, you can't feel good. Therefore, bullying generates unhappiness." "Well," Mom says. "That's the way it seems to be. But it is the other way around. The bullying itself doesn't makes us feel what we feel. It's what we *think* bullying is and what we think about bullying that makes us feel what we feel. So we make our own sadness. We *feel* what we *think*. Our experience is created from the inside out. It doesn't come from outside."

"Hmm ..." Izzy ponders. "It sounds weird." "It does," says Mom. It really seems to be the other way, doesn't it? Just like the sun, it definitely seems as though it's moving. Yet it isn't. And this is the same." "Do I have to learn to enjoy bullying?" Izzy asks with a startled look on her face. "Certainly not," Mom answers. "We'll talk about that later.

First, let's take a few steps back. Forget everything you know. Throw everything that you've ever learned in that big toy box over there. All your thoughts. Even the ones about bullying and things like that. Then I'll start telling you about the three laws. They explain how your life works." "Alright," Izzy says. She crawls back under the duvet. With an empty head. Mom starts to speak.

"The three laws of life are Mind, Consciousness and Thought. You don't need to remember those names, though. The word 'law' might sound a bit odd," Mom says. "As if someone has made them up. That's not the case. You can't make up laws like these. But you can discover them and name them. A law simply explains how something works," Mom says. "And it's very convenient to know how something works. Because then you can take those rules into account and then use them for your benefit."

"There are laws in nature, too. For example, the law of gravity. Have you been taught that in school yet? To keep it simple: that law says that everything falls down. Of course, everybody has always known this. You can see it. And feel it too, if you trip over! But why this is so, has been a mystery for a long time. Isaac Newton found it out by coincidence. When an apple fell out of a tree. He sat under that tree and suddenly he knew: 'There's a force on earth which does this! Gravity.' Newton studied physics. He wrote down what he had discovered. How it worked and why. So other people could use it. For example, when someone wanted to build a plane and didn't want to crash."

"The law of gravity applies to everybody. Even newborn babies. They've never heard of gravity, of course. But still, if their mothers dropped them, they wouldn't float, they would fall to the floor. That's why such a law is called a law. Because it applies to every person here on on earth. It's true even if you don't know anything about it. And gravity is quite convenient, by the way. Otherwise we would all be floating up to the ceiling all the time!" Mom laughs.
"Now that would be super cool" thought Izzy, "floating around together". She could see the picture clearly in her mind. Spike hanging up in the air, frantically snapping at chewy dog treats floating by.

When they finished laughing Mom continued, "The three laws that I talk about were discovered over thirty years ago by a man named Sydney Banks. A Scottish man who lived in Canada. Just like Newton, he suddenly understood how things worked. Life, who we are as human beings and why we experience life the way we do. These laws apply to every single person. But not everyone knows how it works and why. It's very handy when you DO know how it works. Just like it's nice to know that things always fall down because of gravity. You can take it into account. So you won't be surprised every time something falls down. And you know you'd better use the stairs when you go down, instead of jumping." Izzy nods. That's a lot smarter, indeed.

Then she suddenly asks "But you never call them laws, do you mom? You use another word. Popsicles or something like that. It says so on the sign in the waiting room." Mom laughs. "Popsicles, that sounds nice! That's what we'll call them from now on. The Three Popsicles. You're right, I don't say laws. I call them Principles. It means the same." "But grown-ups like to make it complicated, I guess," says Izzy. "Yes," Mom laughs, "it sounds a lot better and it looks pretty interesting on my business cards, too!"

"But the two of us will call them The Three Popsicles now. And I think this is enough for today. You now know what a law is. You know there are three laws for life. You know that your thoughts create your feelings. And that a lot of people turn that around," Mom concludes her story.

Izzy nods. "I still don't get it, though." "You don't need to get this, honey," Mom soothes her. "You'll just start to feel it. We'll continue tomorrow, if you want to, of course. Sleep well, dear." "You too," Izzy whispers. She's almost asleep. Everything she knows is still in her toy box. It feels nice and quiet now.

CHAPTER 4

Izzy is the toaster

The next morning Mom, Dad and Izzy are having breakfast. "I'd like some toast!" Izzy says. "Me too," Dad says. He puts two slices of bread in the toaster. One for Izzy and one for himself. He presses down the handle. Dad also makes a cup of tea and some coffee for Mom, with hot milk. The tea is ready in no time. The coffee too. Dad puts everything on the table. Izzy is waiting for the toaster to go 'ping'. It takes a long time. Much too long. And Izzy's stomach is rumbling. She gets up and walks over to the counter top. "Dad, the toaster light isn't on!" she says. Dad comes and takes a look. "Haha," he laughs. "It's still unplugged! Now that's silly. No wonder it's not working!" Now Izzy sees it too. She puts the plug into the socket. The light goes on immediately. Soon Izzy smells the wonderful scent of freshly toasted bread.

"That's what I'm going to talk to you about tonight," mom suddenly says. "About toast?" Izzy is puzzled. "No, about Mind, remember? The first of the three popsicles? It's energy or a sort of electricity!" Mom says. "Without electricity, the toaster doesn't work. And without this special energy you don't work!" "So I'm a toaster!" Izzy shrieks. Mom and Dad are doubling up with laughter. 'Ping!' goes the toaster.

"I'm all warmed up now!" Izzy calls. She carefully fishes the slices of bread out of the toaster. She puts them on two plates and gives one to Dad. The other one she puts on her side of the table. Izzy sits down and puts butter and cheese on the toast. It starts melting a little bit. Delicious! But now she has to hurry up. Nina will soon be there to pick her up. School's waiting.

That night it's time for Mom's laws. Izzy is tired. She's had a long day at school. Afterwards, she walked with Spike. Then she played outside with Nina. The sun was shining brightly. Or ... well ... there weren't any clouds. They stayed outside until dinner. Then Izzy had some homework to do. She didn't finish her sums at school. Dad helped her and then they were solved quickly. Finally, Izzy was allowed to play with the video game console. She decided to play a game of Mario. Next week she's going to stay with Nan for a couple of days, who's really good at gaming. So Izzy wanted to practice. Perhaps she can beat her Nan for a change.

Now she's lying comfortably in her cosy bed after a lovely, hot bath. Mom plumps down in the pink beanbag again. She starts to talk about energy. "This is something that I can't show you," mom says. "You can feel it, but you can't touch it. That 'something' gives life to everything. People have always known this. They have *felt* it. It has been given hundreds of different names. You probably know a few of them. Some people call it God, for example. The Indians call it 'Big Mind', I think. Some people say 'All-that-is' or 'Mind' or 'Love' or 'Universal Energy'. Let us call it Energy. Nice and simple."

"That's my light!" Izzy calls. "Yes!" Mom nods. "You've named it very well. Anyway, that energy is super, super, super smart. It makes little seeds grow into tall trees. Pine cones become pine trees and not oak trees. Tulip bulbs become tulips. That Energy has made you grow into a human being, from a tiny seed and an egg. This amazing Energy takes care of the seasons, Spring, Summer, Fall and Winter." Izzy nods. She's too tired to say anything. Mom continues.

"The Energy takes care of all things. If you have a little cut on your hand, new skin will grow automatically and cover it. This Energy makes your heart beat, too. You don't need to think about it. Most things your body does are done without your help, aren't they?" Izzy nods again. "And that's very fortunate," Mom says. "Otherwise you would have to keep thinking about making poop out of your breakfast when you're at school! But your body knows how to do that by itself. It has the Energy inside."

That makes Izzy laugh. She can see the picture in her mind. Miss Marion who's explaining how to do long divisions while she herself is busy with producing poop all the time. Mom chuckles at the idea, too. "With animals, we can see the Energy at work with their instincts," Mom explains. "Bears don't have a calendar or a watch. Still, they know when it's time to hybernate. Perhaps they get a signal from the Energy. Smart, isn't it? We as humans have something similar. We have a lot of knowledge inside. We don't need to learn it. We're born with it. It's all inside us already."

"Everything you see around you is powered by the Universal Energy. The sun, the moon and the stars. The earth of course, with all its people and plants and animals. That Energy is everything. It is in everything but you can't see it. Do you understand?" Izzy shrugs. "A little bit," she answers. "but not with my head. It's more like a feeling. It's that light." "That's beautiful," Mom nods. "You don't need to think about this anyway. You don't need to remember my words. It's all about how you feel."

"So. The Energy is a bit like electricity," Mom continues. "You can't see it. You can't grab it. But you can see what the electricity does. It is everywhere and nowhere at the same time. And you need it to make appliances work. The same way you need the Energy to live."

"So I was right!" Izzy giggles. "I'm a toaster." Suddenly she's no longer tired. She's energized! "You're more like a radio," Mom laughs. "With a lot of talk shows!" "I've got music, too!" Izzy says. She starts singing. "Ssssh, you'd better sing a lullaby,"

Mom says. "It's high time you got some sleep now." "My instinct tells me it's not," Izzy states. "Well, then you just stay awake," Mom laughs. "But I'm going downstairs now. Good night, dear." Mom gives Izzy a cuddle. And a kiss on her forehead. And one on her nose. Then Mom disappears from Izzy's room. Down the stairs she goes. Izzy stays awake a little while longer. She breathes in. She breathes out and then notices that it all happens automatically. "How cool," she thinks.

CHAPTER 5

Being Angry is Being Scared

Izzy wakes up early the next morning. She'll have her first guitar lesson that afternoon. She's looking forward to it. It's in a building near her school. She'll go there immediately after school. David, the boy from next door, will be in the same class with her. Izzy doesn't know whether she's happy about that. David can be quite annoying. He's very tall and he has spiky hair. David is in Primary 5 too. At the same school as Izzy. But not in the same class. Fortunately.

At the breakfast table Mom says: "You have a guitar lesson this afternoon, Izzy!" "Yes, it's going to be fun," Izzy says. "Shall I pick you up from school and take you there?" Mom asks. "No," Izzy answers. "That's ok, I already know where it is and I've already met the guitar teacher." "Perhaps you can walk over there with David," Mom suggests. "Yuck," says Izzy. "David is always acting stupidly. He sometimes gives me a push or a punch in the school playground. David seems to be angry all the time. He probably thinks he's cool," Izzy snorts. "No, I prefer to go alone. I wish he wasn't in the same guitar class."

"Hmm ..." Mom muses. "Why would David act like that do you think?" Izzy shrugs. "No idea," she says. "You might try to look at him closely next time,"

Mom suggests. "Look at him? Izzy asks. "And do nothing? Do I have to let myself get punched?" "No, silly," Mom laughs. "Then what am I supposed to do?" Izzy wants to know. "If he does something annoying to me again?" "I don't have an answer to that," Mom says. "At least ... not an answer that's always the right answer. But do you know what's so nice, Izzy? You know what to do yourself. Whatever happens."

"You never tell me what to do," Izzy exclaims. "Nina's Mom always says "You have to say *this*. Or, next time you do *that* ..." "I'm a very lazy mother. I know," Mom laughs. "But you know, Izzy, it would be easy for me to give you advice. I can tell you what to do. But the thing is, sometimes things will happen when I won't be there, so it's good for you to know what to do yourself. You can still speak to me but this way, you won't have to ask me time and again. 'What do I have to do now?' 'And now?' 'And now?' It's much smarter for you to know what to do yourself."

"And I *know* that you know. Just be quiet for a moment. An answer will come. Always. From inside. Because you have all the wisdom of the world inside you. It's that light. The Energy. A little voice that's always around. If you have to run away, you'll know. If you have to ask your teacher for help, you'll know. If you have to scream '*No!!!*' at the top of your lungs, you'll know. Or you'll know what to say to David."

The doorbell rings. "Nina!" Izzy is startled. "Is it that late already?" She hasn't even finished her breakfast. Fortunately, Dad just made her a smoothie. With banana, apple and cucumber. It's really tasty. Mom opens the door for Nina. Izzy pours the smoothie into a take away cup. So she can drink it on her way to school.

Nina's wearing a new pair of jeans. With embroidered flowers on her back pocket. She proudly shows them. Izzy thinks they're really beautiful. "Cool!" she says. Nina has been her best friend for a very long time. They went to a playgroup together. Nina lives two blocks away, near the park. She is slightly taller than Izzy and she has brown hair. It's really curly. Her eyes are brown as well. Nina has two little sisters. They're twins and their names are Jolene and Mara. The twins are five years old. Izzy thinks the little girls are very cute. She loves to go over to Nina's house. Sometimes they play school. Nina and Izzy are the teachers. They teach the twins how to write words. Or they go to the park with Nina's mother. That's fun too.

Now they have to go, otherwise they'll be late. Izzy grabs her schoolbag and her breakfast. She gives Mom a quick kiss. "See you later!" Mom is standing at the door, watching them go off. She waves. Izzy and Nina don't see her. "Shall we play together this afternoon?" Nina asks. "I can't. I have a guitar lesson," Izzy answers. She takes a sip of her smoothie. "Oh, I want to learn how to play the guitar too!" Nina says. "Yes, go and ask your Mom," Izzy suggests, "so we can go together!" Nina is not sure whether her parents will agree. She has jazz, ballet lessons and gymnastics practice too. But she could ask.

It's a boring day at school. Izzy secretly draws a rabbit during math. At recess, she bumps into David. "My mother told me you're going to guitar lessons as well!" he says to Izzy. Izzy nods. "I've had three lessons before," David says. "Last year. So I'm much better at it than you are." At first, Izzy feels like snapping at David. But she doesn't. "I guess you are," she says instead. David is quiet. He walks away, muttering something. "Later," Izzy thinks she hears.

Finally, it's half past two. Izzy takes her school bag from the coat rack. She puts on her jacket. It's cold outside. She walks three blocks. First a turn to the left, then twice to the right. There's the community centre where the guitar lessons are being given. Izzy sees David walking in that direction, too. She slows down her pace so he won't notice her. Inside the guitar teacher is waiting for them already. She's wearing small, round glasses. The teacher's name is Amélie. That's French. She's wearing a long, black skirt. Her hair is cut short and dyed purple. Izzy thinks it looks beautiful. The teacher goes to get herself a cup of tea. The children are allowed to go inside the music room and wait for her there.

There are four of them. Izzy sits down on one of the stools. David takes the one next to her. He has a bag of crisps. He takes a few crisps and throws them into the hood of Izzy's sweater. 'Gross,' Izzy thinks. She's just about to open her mouth, when Mom's words come into her mind. She knows what to do. Just be quiet for a moment.

Suddenly, Izzy wriggles her arms out of her sleeves. In one swift move, she turns her sweater around. Now she's got the front side backwards. Izzy puts her arms back into her sleeves again. Her hood is hanging under her chin. "Crisps, how lovely!" she says. She takes two pieces, puts them in her mouth and starts chewing. Then she turns to David, "Thanks! Can I get some more?" David looks puzzled. "Erm ... no," he answers. "Too bad," Izzy smiles. She calmly looks into David's eyes. She's no longer afraid of him. Suddenly she knows, David is scared. Scared to *not* be seen as cool. That's why he acts the way he does. 'That's a pity,' Izzy thinks. 'I feel sorry for him. David's got clouds covering his sun.' She turns her sweater back around again.

Amélie begins. Izzy pays close attention so she'll know what to do later. First, Amélie plays and sings a French song. About a dead rooster or something like that. Yet it's a cheerful tune. It sounds nice. They learn to name all the parts of the guitar. They learn how to hold it. The teacher explains how to play a chord. Your fingers have to be straight on the strings. And then press down firmly on the fret.

Then you pluck. "That's the way to do it," Amélie tells them. One after the other, the children play a chord. Izzy doesn't think about David anymore.

CHAPTER 6

How Does it Feel?

"How was your guitar lesson?" Dad asks. They're sitting at the table. Dad has cooked pasta and serves it with a delicious salad. Izzy has just taken a mouthful. "It was fun!" she mumbles. "My guitar teacher is really nice. She can play very funny songs. We've learned to play a chord and we have to practice at home." Izzy is allowed to play on Dad's guitar. She hasn't got one herself yet. If she really enjoyes playing, she will get her own guitar. Dad is very good at playing the guitar. Izzy wants to be as good as he is.

At half past eight, Mom walks upstairs with Izzy, who has taken a shower earlier. Mom begins to talk. "Today the second law," she says. "Universal Consciousness. A difficult word. Let's call it Experience. Do you know what that means?" "Sure," Izzy nods. "I'm experiencing cold feet at the moment." Mom smiles. "That's exactly right," she says. "It's the fact that you can see, hear, feel, smell, taste and touch. It's the law that says we can be conscious of everything. It's when we feel we're alive. And perceive what's in our life. We use our senses to interpret the Energy. We have ears, eyes, a nose, our skin and a tongue. And our feelings inside. Through all these senses we experience life.

And isn't that great? That we can see your drawings? And each other? And beautiful movies? And flowers and trees and the sea?"

Izzy nods. Now Mom really gets going. "Isn't it fantastic that we're able to smell the sea? And freshly cut grass?" "Yes," Izzy giggles. "And Spike's turds. And Dad's explosions!" "Those too," Mom laughs. "Wonderful, isn't it? You can feel the softness of Spike's fur." "And my velvet chair at Nan's house!" Izzy shrieks. "And we can hear beautiful music," Mom continues, "but also the horrible sound of fingernails on a blackboard." "Mom, we have digital blackboards at school." Izzy rolls her eyes. Mom's falling behind. "That's true, you're right," Mom chuckles. "Nice and quiet."

Mom thinks for a second. "Ah yes," she says. "When we're watching a sad part of a movie. Like when Bambi loses his mom. We cry sometimes. At least I do. What you feel then, is 'experiencing' too. You feel good or you feel angry. You feel happy or scared. Without experience you wouldn't notice that you're alive. Think about it. How would it be if you didn't see or hear anything? If you couldn't feel anything on your skin? Didn't have feelings inside you? Couldn't taste nor smell anything? You wouldn't be alive," Mom says.

"So everybody experiences something. But *how* you experience and *what* you experience? That's different for every single human being. It's personal.

That's what we call it. For every person it's different. And your experience varies all the time, too. If I'm very happy when I'm vacuuming the house, I may sing a song. I like to vacuum in that moment. If I'm angry and I'm vacuuming, I don't enjoy it at all. The vacuuming is still the same. But the experience is different. It's not the fault of the vacuuming. It's my mood. And when we start talking about moods, we need to take a look at the third law."

"The third law, Thought, makes it so that you *know* what you're experiencing. It enables you to give it a name. Hot or cold. Yummie or yuck. And it also lets you know how you're experience something. What you think about it. Whether you are happy or scared or angry. Like with the vacuum cleaning, thought creates your feelings. So what you feel is your thinking in that moment and not something outside of you. We'll talk about that tomorrow. "You will have to think about it a while, I think," Izzy laughs. Mom can't help but laugh, too. "No," she says. "I think as little as possible. That way I know a lot more." Izzy doesn't get that. But she's heard enough for now.

"I'm going to read for a while," she says. "Fine," Mom nods. "I'm going to take nice hot bath. Sleep well, darling." "Have a nice bath, Mom," Izzy says. She grabs a book from her night stand. It's a 'How to draw Manga' book. Manga comes from Japan. It's a certain style of drawing comic characters. The

Japanese way. Izzy thinks the images are beautiful. She looks at the drawings for a long time. Then she falls asleep. With the book on her face.

CHAPTER 7

Madness and a Moustache.

The next day is Friday. The last day before half-term holiday. They're going to do some fun stuff at school. Everyone is allowed to come dressed-up. Izzy has put her painter's overalls over her clothes. Nice and easy. She doesn't like dressing up that much. Izzy's eating a cheese sandwich and Mom has made her a smoothie. It's green and quite tasty. Mom always adds some nuts, which Izzy really likes. When she's finished with her breakfast, Izzy looks at the kitchen clock. It's five minutes past eight. Nina will soon be here. Izzy doesn't need to take her school bag today. School will be out around lunch time. She brushes her teeth. Then it's ten past eight. Nina should be here now. At a quarter past eight, Nina still hasn't arrived. Izzy decides to give her a call. Perhaps Nina is ill. Izzy picks up the telephone and presses 'Memory 5'. That's Nina's number.

Nina's mother answers the phone. "Hello, this is Izzy," Izzy says. "Is Nina ill? She's not here yet." "Oh," Nina's mother replies. "Didn't she tell you? Nina went cycling to school today, with Caitlin, the new girl from next door. She ..." Izzy interrupts her. "She hasn't said anything about that." "I'm sorry to hear that, Izzy," Nina's mother says. "You'd better

get going then. Otherwise you'll be late for school."
"Yes," Izzy answers glum-ly. "Thank you."

Tears well up in her eyes. Is Nina mad at her or something? Or perhaps she DID tell that she wasn't coming? Izzy's fairly sure she didn't. And if Nina had told her, she still thinks it's stupid. They always go to school together, don't they? They're best friends, aren't they? Does Nina suddenly think that girl Caitlin is nicer than she is? All of a sudden, Izzy doesn't feel like going to school to play games anymore. She feels sad.
Mom sticks her head around the corner of the kitchen wall. "So, is Nina ill?" "No." Izzy shakes her head. "She went to school with someone else. On her bicycle and she didn't say anything about it to me." Izzy sobs. "I don't get it! We haven't had a fight. I didn't say anything mean to Nina either." Now Izzy's getting angry. "It's not fair! She can't do things like this! We always go together!" Mom is quiet. Izzy feels herself calm down a bit. "Actually, I don't care. Let them do what they want. And who IS that Caitlin anyway? I don't know anyone called Caitlin. It's probably some dumb girl."
Mom still doesn't say anything. She holds Izzy in her arms and strokes her hair. That feels nice. "Perhaps there is a simple expla-nation for this" Mom soothes her. "We can't possibly know." Izzy takes a deep breath. "I could ask Nina," she says. "That's a good idea" Mom nods. "I guess I had better go now" Izzy sighs. She's too late already.

Izzy drags herself to school. She still feels a bit sad. She thinks about what Mom said last night. About thoughts. What was that again? They make you feel the way you do. That's it. 'I feel sad,' Izzy knows. 'What thoughts do I have? I think Nina doesn't like me anymore. I think she doesn't want to be friends any longer. I think she didn't tell me anything on purpose. I think Nina is betraying me. I think it's stupid. Well ... no wonder I feel sad and angry. What madness!' Izzy can't help but laugh about herself now. In the meantime, she has arrived at school. The school yard is almost empty. All the children have gone inside already. Izzy walks to her classroom. She takes off her coat and hangs it on the coat rack. There's a lot of noise coming from inside the classroom. Miss Marion has put on some music. A lot of children are dancing and prancing around. There are board games on the tables. Nobody has noticed that Izzy's late.

Izzy steps into the classroom. There's Nina talking to a new girl. The girl is quite short and has blonde hair, cut short. She's dressed up as a pirate. Nina and the little pirate are laughing out loud now. 'Are they talking about me?' Izzy wonders. She takes a deep breath and walks towards the two girls. Nina turns around. She's smiling. "Caitlin, this is Izzy," says Nina. "My best friend in the whole world." "Hi," Caitlin greets her. "Hi," says Izzy. "Why didn't you come and pick me up this morning?" Izzy asks. "I left a message on your answering machine this morning," Nina answers with eyes as big as saucers. "Didn't you get it?" "Oh ... well ... no," Izzy says. "Caitlin moved into the house three doors down from ours," Nina starts explaining. "She'll be in our class, too! Today is her first day. Her mother asked me if I could go with her this morning. Her parents suddenly had to go to the hospital." "My grandpa is ill," Caitlin says. Nina continues, "Her mother thought that it was a bit sad for Caitlin to go to school all on her own on her first day at a new school. So she came over to our house very early this morning. I immediately called you. But nobody answered the phone." "We were still upstairs, I guess," Izzy says. What she's hearing now is different from what she thought what was going on.

The classroom party lasts the entire morning. There's lemonade and muffins. There are little sticks with fruit. They eat and drink and dance. Izzy plays Monopoly and Twister. It's quite a nice day. School's out at noon. It's half-term! Izzy is going to have a sleepover at Nan's house. She's really looking forward to that.

Dad is waiting for her in the schoolyard. Spike is sitting at his feet. Izzy runs outside. She cuddles her dog. "I've already taken a walk with Spike," Dad says. "So we can head straight home. Or do you have a play date with anyone?" Izzy sees Nina and Caitlin leaving together. On their bikes. She shakes her head. "No, I'm going with you." She feels a bit jealous of little Caitlin. "Shall we have lunch in town?" Dad proposes. Izzy thinks that's a wonderful idea. "I want to take off my overalls first though," she states. "No problem," says Dad. "We'll have to take Spike home anyway."

They're home in no time at all. Mom is there, too. "How was the party at school?" she asks Izzy. "Okay, I guess," Izzy replies, shrugging her shoulders. "Nina was on our voicemail by the way," Mom says. "She called to say she couldn't come to collect you. Have you spoken to her?" Izzy nods. She has. And she still feels a bit 'off' when she thinks about it.

Then Mom says: "My client for this afternoon has cancelled. Shall we go and have lunch in town? To celebrate your holiday?" Dad laughs. "Exactly my idea! How nice that you can join us too." Izzy runs up the stairs to take off her overalls. Going out for lunch with Mom and Dad is fun. What food will she order in the restaurant? A cheese toastie? A cheese omelette? Izzy loves cheese. "I'm ready to go!" she calls out once she's downstairs again.

Dad has got his old cargo tricycle from the shed. Izzy climbes into the cargo tub, with a pillow under her bottom because the tub is hard. And the greater part of their route has little cobblestones.

It's rather busy in the town centre. Dad, Mom and Izzy arrive at the restaurant. They've been here before. It looks really cozy, with long benches lining the walls, big fluffy pillows and a huge fireplace. A fire is burning. The three of them sit down in a quiet corner of the restaurant. They look at the menu. Dad feels like a salad. Mom orders a bowl of soup. Izzy chooses an omelette. While they're waiting for their food, Izzy looks around.

Next to them, there's a man sitting alone at a table. He has taken his computer tablet with him. He's looking at it the whole time. Izzy can see he's reading his emails. One of the messages is making him smile. Reading the next message, the man looks angry. At another message he sighs deeply. Sometimes he's drumming on the table with his fingers. His feet move restlessly. Dad would call it 'Nerdvously.' Now and then, the man takes a bite from his toastie. Or he sips his tea. He seems not to be tasting any of it. He's too caught up in all his mail.

"Mom," says Izzy. "Have you seen the man sitting next to us?" Mom hasn't noticed him. She was too busy talking with Dad. Now she glances sideways. "It's so funny," Izzy says. "Nothing is happening. That man is just sitting here. With a toastie and a cup of tea. Looking at his tablet. But there seems to be a lot going on. I've seen him get happy first. And then angry. And then 'nerdvous'. Isn't that a bit strange?" Mom nods. "everything is happening inside his head. His thoughts are changing all the time. And everytime they give a different feeling. A completely different world, it seems. It's all his thinking."

Izzy lowers her voice. She puts on a very serious face. With her finger pointing in the air she slowly states: "When you've got too much thinking, you don't notice what you're eating or drinking!" Mom and Dad explode with laughter. "That's so true!" Mom cries. Then the waiter arrives with their food. "Attack!" Izzy says. She's not thinking about anything anymore. She wants to taste her omelette.

"I have another reason to celebrate," Dad says a little bit later. "We've received a large assignment. Building new programmes for game consoles. I immediately gave my staff the rest of the day off to celebrate!" "That's the reason you were home so early today!" Mom says. "How cool!" Dad nods. His blue eyes were shining with delight. 'The next few months we'll have to play really hard!" he beams. Dad never says he has to work. He calls it 'playing'. Because he loves his job so much. "I think I'm going to ask Nan to work with me," Dad says. "To test our new games." Mom and Izzy have to laugh. Nan would enjoy that very much, they think. Nan just loves gaming.

"Can't you build me a programme sometime soon?" Izzy asks. "To put into my head? A math pro-gramme?" "You are much smarter than a computer," Dad laughs. "Everything that comes out of a computer, you have to put in first. Like in your brains. But we humans can do something far better. We can get new ideas." Aren't those coming from my brain, too?" Izzy asks, puzzled. "I don't think so," answers Dad. "If you're really quiet in your head, you get the best ideas. I always say you're on-line then. Connected to a kind of universal internet containing all knowledge." "I'd like to have a subscription," Izzy says. "So I'll have all the answers to my sums." "What about using a calculator?" Dad suggests. "That's not allowed, my teacher says," Izzy answers gloomily. "And now I got an F on my report card." "No sweat, Izzybusy," Dad soothes her. "There are other subjects you excel in." "We'll discuss it with Miss Marion," Mom says. "Maybe we can arrange something." Izzy nods. She's happy. It would be great if she could use a calculator.

When they've finished eating their meal, the three of them order hot chocolate with whipped cream, of course. After all, they have two things to celebrate. Izzy has a creamy moustache. And so has Dad. Now he has two moustaches. "Well, look at my handsome family!" Mom chuckles. They pay the bill. Outside, Izzy jumps into the cargo tub of the tricycle again. She's still wearing her creamy moustache. Dad keeps his as well. On their way home they wave at everyone. Most people wave back. They see some people they know. "How are you doing?" their neighbour Joseph asks. "Splendid!" Dad shouts. "I'd love to stay and chat, but I really moustache!" Izzy has a giggling fit.

CHAPTER 8

All About Lights

That night Izzy goes to bed really late. She doesn't have to get up early the next morning anyway. In fact, she can sleep in the entire week! "Do you want to hear about the third law?" Mom asks. "Of course!" Izzy grins. She's not tired yet. Together they go upstairs. Mom lies down on the bed beside her. "Fine. The third law," Mom begins. "Thought!" Izzy says. "Indeed," Mom nods "Thought is a beautiful gift. You colour your world with it."

"Just like when I'm drawing?" Izzy asks. "Sort of," says Mom. "Let me see. The white piece of paper is life. Pure Energy without form. You need the paper to make a drawing. But it doesn't have colour in and of itself. It's neutral, we say. It doesn't mean anything. Then there's your colouring pencils. Thought. Your thinking guiding your hands. Creating something on the piece of paper. You draw something beautiful, or you draw an ugly picture. That's up to you. It's your drawing. It reflects the ideas you have inside you. They go from inside you to the outside world. On your piece of paper." Izzy can see the picture. "Oh, *that*'s what you meant with 'living inside out'!"
"Yes!" Mom says. "That's right. Well. About the drawing. Every person has a different preference.

Some people like black and white and grey. Others prefer bright colours. Red, blue, yellow, green, orange. One isn't better than the other. It's up to you what you like and choose. "You see your drawing through your own eyes, you experience it?" asks Izzy. "Yes, something like that," Mom says.

"With my pencils I create drawings, with my thinking I create my life," Izzy contemplates. "Your reality," Mom nods. "Then I'll use the most beautiful colours I can find!" Izzy says. "Of course!" Mom cries. "You pick the colours that you like. That make you feel good. It's quite funny, actually," Mom continues. "people often scare themselves with their own thoughts. That's like drawing a monster, getting scared looking at it. And then run away screaming." "Hahaha," Izzy laughs. She sees what Mom means.

Once they're done laughing, Mom goes on. "It's sad actually, when people don't know they can choose their own colours. Most people think the world is just 'out there'. That one can only look at the drawing, so to speak. And judge it and then feel something about it. I call that 'living from the outside in'. If you know about the three popsicles, you see it works in a different way. That you're creating the drawing yourself. You're living from the inside out." Izzy gets it.

"There are different ways of thinking," mom continues. "Just like there are different ways of drawing. You can simply draw what comes up. That's how you usually do it, right?" Izzy nods. That's the way she likes to do it. Those drawings always turn out beautifully. "Is that the inspiration that Nan is always talking about?" "Exactly!" Mom cries out. "Inspiration. Well said. It's a thought from Universal Energy. I call it 'big thinking'. It produces wonderful new things."

"You can also copy something," Mom says. "Like when your teacher says: 'draw a square! Or you have to trace a drawing made by someone else. Then everybody has to do the same." "Copycatting," says Izzy. "Sooooo boring!" Mom laughs. "Yes. And those are 'little thoughts'. The thinking of your little 'me'. What you've learned from others."

Izzy and her Mom are quiet for a while. "I know the difference when I'm drawing," Izzy finally says. "But how's that working in my head? How do I know whether my thinking is big or little?" "You can *feel* it." Mom replies. "Just like when you're drawing. Inspiration feels nice and free. Copying feels boring. Big Thought gives a nice feeling. You're happy and content. Little thinking generates angry or sad feelings."

"That's right!" Izzy suddenly remembers, "sometimes I'm bored to death. I don't feel like doing anything. Everything seems to be stupid. I feel 'yucky'. Then sometimes, I go and lie quietly on my bed for a while. It feels as if I'm falling asleep. And right at that moment, I suddenly know what I want. It's more like falling awake! And it comes with a happy feeling. I picture a nice drawing in my mind. With all the colours and shapes. And I immediately jump up to make that drawing. Or I don't see anything, but I just feel like drawing. Or I feel like taking Spike over to Nina. Or I want to play a game on the computer. Or I feel like going into the garden and jumping on the trampoline. Or watch a movie, or ... something always pops up!"

Mom nods. "I can tell I don't need to explain this to you." "But those little thoughts. How about them?" Izzy asks. "Do I need to stop having them?"
"Well," Mom begins, "that's not really possible. Everybody has those thoughts. It's part of being human. But it's nice to know how it works. With the three principles, I mean popsicles, it makes things easier. You know," Mom says, "there has *never* been someone who had very happy thoughts and still felt sad. Nor has there ever been someone who had very angry thoughts who still felt wonderful. It's just impossible."
Again, they're quiet. Then Mom says: "Your feelings will always tell you where your thinking is. It's a beautiful system, Just like the warning lights in a car. If they're off, all is well. You feel good. But when a red light is blinking, you might want to pull over and stop. The red light in a car is not 'wrong'. It's handy. A yucky feeling isn't 'wrong' either. It's simply a signal of where your thinking is. Nothing more. Nothing less."

"Some grown-ups don't want to feel bad," Mom says. "They ignore their feelings. That's the same as putting a sticker on the warning light in your car. Not so smart. You keep going while the red light is blinking. Because you can't see it. And then people get stuck. They don't pay attention to what they feel and think." "That's what happened to Nina's Dad," Izzy remembers. "What did he call it? A burn out. I guess his motor was on fire. He must not have been paying attention to his warning light!" Mom nods in agreement.

"But ... I don't need to change my thoughts? Izzy asks. "Nope," Mom smiles. "That would be very tiresome, wouldn't it? Every time you have a stupid thought, you'd have to work on it. It's a nice trick, though. It works sometiems, too. For a little while. But the easiest way is to know how life works. With the three popsicles you might laugh about such thoughts. Or you don't do anything with them. You don't even believe them. You might wait until they pass. Thoughts don't have any power over you. Unless you start paying a lot of attention to them, of course. But you don't *have* to. It's your choice."

This all sounds quite relaxed to Izzy. It feels good anyway. She knows that's the only thing that's important. "Feeling good. Calm. Happy. And if you don't feel like that, there's no problem. How you feel will automatically change, when you wait quietly for a new thought." explains Mom.

"So ... if you live by these three laws, you'll be happier," Izzy states. "Everybody lives by these laws," Mom says. "People who are always angry. People who are often sad, too. The thing is, they just do not know it. It's just like gravity, remember? You don't need to think all the time, today I'm going to use gravity. I'm going to make sure I won't float off into space." Izzy giggles. "But," Mom continues, "if you understand how it works, life is easier. Because you know. When I'm sad or angry, it's a thought. And it'll pass. Nothing needs to be done. Of course, things will happen around you. But you look at them differently. You know that you are colouring or creating those things with thought. From the inside out, and not the other way around. And you *know* you have the Energy within. Your light, as you call it. With all solutions, with inspiration, with new, fresh thoughts. So you can feel you're always okay. Inside. That your 'light' is always shining. Even when there are many clouds around. They will pass. Or they change shape. You don't take life so seriously. No matter what seems to happen. You worry less and that's nice."

Izzy nods. "Just like you, I guess. You're never worried." "I'm a bit worried now," Mom jokes. "I fear I'll still be laying here until tomorrow morning!" She gets up and gives Izzy a big hug. "Sleep well, dear." "Good night, Mom." Then Mom goes downstairs. Izzy lies awake for a little while longer. She's thinking about what Mom has said. She doesn't need to remember any of it. Izzy knows, 'everything is okay, whatever happens. I'm a shining light. And I'll always notice when my 'car light' is red. It goes on automatically, because I can feel it.'

CHAPTER 9

Nan Takes a Bath

The next day is Saturday. And it's half-term. Izzy is going to stay with her Nan. They always have a lot of fun together. Nan is Dad's mother. Dad is an only child, just like Izzy. Nan is an artist. She has a studio in her back garden. It used to be just a big shed but then Grandpa put in large windows and made it beautiful inside. Grandpa is in heaven now, but the studio is still there. Nan is very pleased with it. She makes huge paintings. Sometimes they're just as tall as Nan herself, with a lot of colours. Izzy thinks they're wonderful. Nan used to paint in the house. It was a big mess. There were paint brushes and tubes of paint everywhere. Now everything is in the studio. Nan gives workshops and lessons there too. For Izzy and for grown-ups.

Sometimes, Nan has an exhibition. She hangs her paintings in a gallery. People come and look at them. Often Nan sells a few canvases. That's what she calls her paintings, canvases. Because that's the sort of fabric she paints on, Izzy thinks.

On Izzy's fourth birthday, Nan told her: "I have a surprise for you! I bought you an easel!" Izzy's eyes were as big as saucers. "A weasel, Nan? Where is it?" Izzy had run outside, looking for a cage. She couldn't find it. So she went back in and asked Nan, "Can I take it home? What does it eat? Does it have a name?" Then Nan had laughed real hard. "I said an *easel*, Isabella! You use it to put your paintings on." Izzy had been a bit dissapointed. She would have loved to have had a pet weasel. But now it turned out she got a little wooden rack to put a canvas on. But that was sort of nice, too. From then on, Izzy was allowed to make paintings in Nan's studio. First she used finger paint. But soon she learned to paint with real brushes and water colours and oil paint. She's quite good at it now. In Nan's studio, there's always a pair of overalls for Izzy. On her own little hook on the wall.

Mom and Dad take her over to Nan's place this Saturday morning. Spike is going with her. First they stop at the bakery to buy a delicious cake. At the florist, they choose a nice bouquet of roses for Nan. Nan lives fairly close by. Izzy will soon be able to go there by herself. On her bike. She sometimes cycles the route with Mom and Dad. But now she has a large bag with her, containing her pyjamas and clean clothes and her toothbrush. And Spike will stay at Nan's too. So his dog pillow has to be brought over. Izzy will stay with Nan for four days. She's really looking forward to it. Especially to painting together. And eating chips. And going out for dinner. Nan doesn't like cooking, she hardly ever cooks. "Way too much trouble, child!" she always says. "Come on, let's go and have some pancakes at the end of the street." Nan lives near the nicest pancake restaurant in the world. With sashed windows and a thatched roof. Nan's house looks the same.

They arrive after a ten minute drive. Dad opens the tailgate of their car. Spike jumps out the car and dashes towards Nan's front door. Nan has dog chewies too and Spike knows, of course. Nan has opened the door already. She's wearing her painter's outfit. Overalls covered with smudges and splashes of paint. Spike jumps up on her. Nan pets him on the head. "There you are, wild animal," she laughs. Then Nan spreads her arms wide out to embrace Izzy. "Isabella! So good to see you!" She lifts Izzy up from the ground and swings her around. "We're going to have fun, dear," Nan says. "You're allowed to stay up all night. We're going to eat cupcakes in bed. And of course, we're going to play games together!" Nan has a lot of different games. Sometimes she's busy playing all night long. Alone, or together with her girl friends. Izzy thinks her Nan is really cool. Nobody has a grandmother like hers. "And painting, Nan!" Izzy beams. "Absolutely," Nan nods and she pulls Izzy inside the house. "Can we come in too?" Dad jokes. "Well ... okay then," Nan says. "But you can't stay very long. Izzy and I have a busy schedule." "We've brought you some cakes," Dad says. "Oh, in that case you can come in to have a cup of coffee," Nan says. They all go inside laughing. Izzy sits down in her very own chair. It's big and soft and covered with purple velvet. She loves the touch of velvet. Nan gives her a cup of hot chocolate and a piece of apple cake. Spike puts his big head on Izzy's lap. He looks at her with begging eyes. "No, Spike," says Izzy. "No cake for you. Nan wil get you a dog chewy later on." Spike immediately runs into the kitchen. Like a good dog, he sits down and waits patiently. 'Smart dog,' Izzy thinks. Mom, Dad and Nan chat for a long time. Izzy wants to paint. "Can I go to the studio now, Nan?" she asks "Of course, dear," Nan replies. "I'll be there in a minute. As soon as I have gotten rid of these parents of yours." "All right, all right, we get the hint," Dad laughs. He gets up from the couch. "Come darling," he says to Mom. "The ladies want to get started on their art work." Izzy gives her parents a big hug. "See you in a couple of days!" she sings as she runs out into the garden, towards the studio.

Her overalls are waiting for her. There's a big white canvas on her easel. Ready to be painted on. Izzy puts on the overalls. She already knows what she's going to create. A painting with only forms and colours. That's called an 'abstract.' You can't see what it is. Izzy gathers everything she needs. Many different colours of paint. A pallette to put the paint on. That's a small wooden board with a hole to put her thumb in. She takes big brushes and small ones. Feathers and a sort of comb. She finds a piece of cloth to smudge paint and a sponge. With all these things she can put the paint on her canvas in many different ways. Izzy start with a big blue streak. It's a beautiful arch. Thick at the beginning and thin at the end. Very soon, Izzy is absorbed by her work.

Nan enters the studio. "Right," she says. "And now to work!" Nan is working on a small painting this time. Izzy sees two women on Nan's canvas. A big one and a small one. "Is that us, Nan?" she points. Nan tilts her head. She looks. "Hmm ... could be," she hesitates. "This is an assignment. But I haven't figured it out yet. I haven't seen an image yet," Nan says. Izzy knows what she means. Nan has explained it to her. Before Nan makes a painting, she already sees how it has to turn out. Not really, of course. But in her mind's eye. She sees an image and that's what she paints. "It's an automatic process," Nan told Izzy. "My hands do the work. I don't have to think about it," she said. Izzy knows what she means. Sometimes she paints that way. And other times she simply begins. Without an image in her head. Then the painting grows, like it does now.

Much, much later, Izzy takes a step back. She looks at her canvas. It's like an explosion of colours. Or fireworks maybe. Izzy is very content. She realizes she's hungry. And thirsty, too. She turns towards Nan. Nan's sitting on a little three-legged stool. Staring at her canvas. Nothing much has changed there, Izzy notices. Nan sighs. "It's not working," she says. "Shall we make toasties?" "Yesss," Izzy cheers. Together they go inside the house. Nan makes cheese toasties. Izzy suddenly thinks about

Mom's story. About the Energy. "Have you heard about the three popsicles, Nan? I mean, those three laws?" Izzy asks. "Oh yes, Isabella!" Nan answers. She's putting the toasties and tea on the table. Izzy immediately attacks the food. "Your Mom explained them to me. And in fact, I already knew it. That Energy also pops all ideas for my painting into my head. But today, it wasn't there, I guess." "That's impossible," Izzy mumbles with her mouth full. "The Energy's always present." "Hmm, I guess you're right about that," Nan says. "But my connection was lost for a moment." "Your internet connection failed!" Izzy giggles. "I'll have to restart it, I think," Nan laughs.

That afternoon, Izzy and Nan take a long walk with Spike. There's no forest near Nan's house but there's a river with a path alongside it. Spike loves it there. The whole way, he's sniffing for new scents. Izzy finds a stick which she throws at least a hundred times and Spike fetches it a hundred times. Izzy talks about her guitar lessons. Nan is pleasantly surprised. "How wonderful," she says. "Perhaps you'll play in a band one day! Just like your Dad used to do. It's so nice to be able to play music. I regret that I've never learned how to play the piano. I think that would have been fun." "Well, you could take lessons now," Izzy suggests. "Yes!" Nan says. "What a wonderful idea. Perhaps I'll buy a piano. So we can play together!"

After their walk it's time to go to the pancake restaurant. It has started to rain. Big raindrops rattle against the small windows. Inside, it's warm and cozy. And so much fun with Nan. Izzy has an apple pancake. She puts a lot of syrup on it. And sugar powder. The pancake is *so* big, she can't eat a dessert. Nan and Izzy run home through the rain.

Izzy takes a DVD from Nan's dresser. She has seen this movie many times already. But it's such a wonderful story! She curles up in her chair. Spike comes and lies down at her feet. Nan decides to take a bath. There are still some traces of paint in her hair. She wants to wash it out. Nan has a bathroom downstairs. She sets the door a little ajar. This way, Izzy and Nan can continue talking while Nan takes her bath. Izzy enjoys that. She hears the water splashing. Then suddenly, the bathroom door flies open. Nan runs into the living room with a towel wrapped around her. Water is dripping from her wet hair. "I've got inspiration!" Nan cries out. She runs into the garden in her bare feet. It's such a funny sight. Izzy has to laugh really hard. Nan's a bit crazy.

When the movie has ended, Izzy walks over to the studio. She looks through the window. There's Nan, painting - only wearing her towel. It's freezing in the studio, but Nan doesn't feel it. There's paint on her bare toes. Nan doesn't notice. When Izzy enters the studio, Nan looks very surprised. "What are you doing here?" Nan asks. Izzy giggles. "I'm staying at your house, Nan!" She knows that Nan forgets everything when she's inspired. "Oh, dear, that's true!" Nan cries out. The painting turned out very beautifully. Nan gives it a satisfied look. "It's finished," she nods. Then she shivers with cold. Suddenly Nan realises she's almost naked. She roars with laughter. "Now I remember ..." she says. "I was lying in the bathtub. I didn't have anything on my mind, certainly not the painting." Izzy cries: "You went online, Nan!" "Yes!" says Nan. "Suddenly, I saw exactly how it had to be done. So now it has been proven again, dear," Nan smiles. "Inspiration comes effortlessly. Do nothing. Just relax and take a bath." "Perhaps I should always carry a bath with me in school," Izzy thinks aloud. "Sounds like a wonderful idea to me," Nan agrees.

Nan turns off the light in the studio. "I'll clean things up tomorrow," she says. They go inside. Nan puts on her warm and comfortable pyjamas. And a bathrobe. Plus a pair of huge rabbit-shaped house shoes. Izzy walks into the spare room. She changes into her pyjamas too. Nan makes tea. They chat for a little while. Nan peels the skin off a pear. She cuts it into little pieces. There are strawberries and raspberries, too. She arranges them onto a plate. Nan makes it look like a painting. Together they savour the fruit.

"Nan, do you miss Grandad often?" Izzy asks. The question just came up. Nan is quiet for a second and then says: "Well, sometimes I do. But you

know, honey, I still talk to him. Like he's here."
"Does he answer you?" Izzy wants to know. Nan
says: "I know Grandad *so* well, that I just know
what he would say. His answers pop into my head.
It is as though he's still here. That's how it feels to
me. I think Grandad is still a piece of the Energy.
He just doesn't have a form anymore. I can't hold
him. That's a pity." Izzy nods. She thinks that's a
pity, too.
"I've been very sad for a while," Nan continues.
"And you know, it was kind of odd. When Grandad
was still alive, I didn't think about him while I was
painting. I just painted. And my mind's empty then.
I gave art classes, just like I do now. I never thought
about Grandad during the lessons. And I went out
with girlfriends. Or game nights. I didn't think
about Gran-dad during those activities.
And then when he died, the only thing I could think
about was Grandad. The whole day, every day! And
you know, I usually don't think much!" Nan laughs.
"It seemed like it was impossible to do anything
different than thinking about Grandad. But after a
while, that changed. I would think about him when
I came home and didn't get a kiss, for instance.
Now I just kiss myself in the mirror," Nan chuckles.
"It's a shame Grandad's gone. If I had the choice, he
would still be here. But that's not the case. I can
choose what I'm focusing on, though. I can look at
what's no longer here and I might get sad. Or I look
at the things that are still here. Like you! And all
the wonderful stories about Grandad. And the
beautiful things he made, like my studio. That feels

a lot better. When I'm sad, it's no problem. I get quiet for a little while. Inside, I mean. Then I notice that the feeling goes away all by itself. I can just feel it and wait." Izzy thinks for a second and then states: "Grandad is a light without a body now." "Exactly," Nan says.

"Shall we play a game of Mario?" Nan suggests. Izzy jumps up. She's definitely in for a game. They go and sit on the couch together, with the controllers in their hands. Nan has a super large screen TV. She easily plays many levels. When Nan conquers in the end, she yells out loud: "Yeaaaaaaaaaaah!" Nan throws her arms up in the air and jumps up to do a silly dance. "You must be practicing very often, Nan," Izzy thinks out loud. Nan nods. "Yes!" she says with a happy face. Izzy's getting a little bit better at it every time she plays. And when her Mario falls off a cliff for the tenth time, she just laughs. It's late when they go to bed. Nan has to brush not only her teeth, but her toes too.

CHAPTER 10

Dreams, Movies and Fights

Four days with Nan fly by. "We've had such a good time!" Nan exclaims when Dad comes to pick up Izzy. "Can't Izzy come and live with me?" Nan asks. "She's so much fun to be with. And you've had her long enough now." Dad has to laugh. "No way," he replies. "Izzy is mine!" Dad picks up Izzy. He throws her over his shoulder and walks to the car. He opens the fifth door. He puts Izzy in the back, in the dog basket. She squeals with laughter. Dad puts Spike in the backseat and buckles him up. Spike looks really confused. That makes Izzy laugh even harder. Dad is doing everything the other way around! Nan has come outside, too. She shakes her head in dismay. "Now you see," Nan says. "You're not fit to be a father. Leave that child with me." Nan frees Izzy from the dog basket. Spike has unwrapped himself from the seatbelt. He jumps right over the backseat into his basket. Izzy sits down behind her father. Everybody is where they belong. All their stuff is already in the car, including a beautiful painting by Izzy. Nan gets one last hug through the car window. Then they drive off. "It was really fun to be with Nan," Izzy sighs. "That's wonderful Izzy-busy," says Dad. Izzy tells him the story about Nan running out of her bathtub. Because she was inspired all of a sudden.

Dad has to laugh. "She sometimes forgot that she had a husband and a child," he chuckles. "She was just too busy painting! And that's how I learned to cook so well," Dad says. "Nan simply lost track of time. Grandpa was often late from work. So I cooked for myself whenever I got hungry." "You enjoy cooking," Izzy says. "Nan doesn't. She thinks it's too much of a hassle." "Ooooh ... you must have eaten a lot of french fries and pancakes as always," Dad laughs. "And a lot of fruit too!" Izzy nods. At home, Mom is standing at the door. She's just saying goodbye to a client. The last one for today. His light is shining brightly, Izzy notices. Mom is very glad to see Izzy again. She hugs her until Izzy is almost choking. Dad immediately walks into the kitchen. He's going to cook something nice. Without meat. Dad and Izzy never eat meat. Mom does, once in a while. Dad sometimes gets her a steak from the biological butcher. He buys his meat from a neighbouring farm. Where the cows are grazing in the meadow. "Then at least I know that the cow has had a good life," Mom says. Izzy thinks it's sad for animals to eat them. And she doesn't like the taste of meat either. Mom does. And she says, "In nature, animals eat each other too. We're part of nature." It sounds logical. Dad has a different opinion about it. "To get one kilo of meat, you have to put thirteen kilos of herbage into a cow," he explained. "We can eat the green food ourselves. Easy peasy. This way, we can use more land to grow food for people. So there's more food for everybody." That sounds true, too. Izzy doesn't really have an idea about it. But she just knows she doesn't want to eat meat.

Izzy remembers she has to play the guitar. To practice chords on Dad's guitar. She doesn't feel like it. She thinks playing chords is a bit boring. She wants to play songs, with Nan and Dad. "First you have to know the basics." Amélie explained to her. And of course, Izzy understands that. Perhaps she'll practice tomorrow. Before she goes to the movies with Mom and Nina. Mom has taken a few days off as well. That's nice.

Izzy has a lot to talk about at the dinner table. She tells them everything about the four days with Nan. "I want to go again next holidays," she sighs. Mom and Dad admire the painting Izzy has made. "I've worked on it for two whole days!" Izzy proudly states. Her parents think it's beautiful. "That blue!" Dad says. "Gorgeous! It resembles the birth of a star. Have you ever seen a picture of that? It's just as beautiful as this. With all the different colours. Can I hang it on one of the walls in my office, Izzy? In the relaxing room?" That sounds cool to Izzy. Dad's office is in a wonderful building. There are a lot of plants. Small trees even. In the space Dad is referring to, there are large, comfortable couches. There's an enormous ball pit. With a spring board. It's fun to 'swim' in. Sometimes Dad has to talk with the people at the office. They meet in the ball pit. "We always get the best ideas there," Dad says. In the cupboards there are pots with clay and finger paint.

Two large walls are covered with blackboards. They are full of drawings, numbers and equations that Izzy doesn't understand. Of course there are a lot of computers there too. It's a computer company after all. They build software. "The thoughts of a computer," Dad explained, "have to be put into the computer, otherwise the computer doesn't know anything. So you could say I fill computers with brains." Sometimes they make computer games too. Those games have to be tested. Then everyone at the office plays games. That's fun. "Can I go with you when you hang up my painting?" Izzy asks. Once in a while, she goes with Dad to his office. "Of course!" Dad replies. "That'll be fun. Shall we say Friday?" Izzy thinks that's fine. "Very well planned," Mom says. "I'm going to go to town with Wendy that day." Wendy is Izzy's Aunt. Mom's sister. Mom has three sisters. Two of them live far away. Wendy's house is in the same town as theirs. She has a nice, big flat on the fifteenth floor. That's the highest. Wendy lives there alone, well, with two cats. They sometimes go and visit Wendy. Izzy likes to look out of the windows there. The view is wonderful! You can see the whole town. The parks and the churches. The forest and the meadows surrounding the town. If the weather is clear, you can even see some villages a couple of miles away.

That night, Izzy is tired. She went to bed very late at Nan's house! "No popsicles tonight?" Mom asks. "No," Izzy shakes her head. "I'm going to sleep right away."

Izzy has a dream. She's walking around in a city. The streets are narrow. Izzy has no idea where she is. Then she hears something behind her. Or someone. She looks around. She can't see anything. It's too dark. Is she being chased? Izzy wants to start running. But her legs are like elastic bands. They just don't work however hard Izzy's trying. She grabs a rope that's hanging from a window. 'I'll climb up,' Izzy thinks in her dream. She knows for *sure* that she can climb very well. At school, she's always one of the first to get up to the ceiling of the gym. Sometimes, she practises in the playground. But now she can't do it. Her arms are like elastic bands, too. Izzy's dangling in the dark. Her heart is pounding in her throat. She hears something approaching. Izzy wants to scream now. And she can!

Suddenly, she's sitting upright in her bed. Mom enters her room. She switches on the light. "Is something wrong, honey?" Mom asks. "I was dreaming," Izzy answers. "It was a nightmare. Someone was chasing me and I couldn't run or climb." Mom sits down beside her. She strokes Izzy's hair and holds her tight for a while. "My heart is beating really fast!" says Izzy. Her legs are trembling. "Yes, isn't that odd?" Mom nods. "In reality, nothing happened. Still, your body tells you something different. It acts as though it wasn't a dream. That's rather clever, don't you think? Just like when you're hungry. If you think about food, your mouth will water." Izzy is calm now. "My body listens to my thoughts," Izzy says. "Also when I'm awake, sometimes I think about a math test. Then I feel a knot in my stomach. Or I think about something really exciting. Then I get butterflies in my belly!"

"That's right," Mom smiles. "And now I'm in my right mind again too," Izzy laughs. She drinks some water. Then she lies down again. Mom gives her a kiss. She walks out of Izzy's room. The light stays on.

Izzy sleeps in late the next morning. It's Thursday. Today Nina's coming over. Mom will take the two of them to a movie. But first, breakfast. Izzy can make her own smoothie. Mom wants one too. Izzy puts spinach leaves in the blender. A banana, an apple, a piece of cucumber and walnuts follow. Plus the orange juice Mom has already pressed. And a handful of those tiny seeds. Izzy puts the lid firmly on the blender. Otherwise she'll spatter the kitchen walls. With a push on the button, the blender grinds all the ingredients. Now it's a green, frothy substance. Izzy pours it into two tall, thick glasses. "Nice!" mom says. Slowly they drink it all. Then they get dressed. Izzy grabs Dad's guitar to practice. She knows how to play three base chords now. A little bit. She finds changing over still a bit tricky. That's going from one chord to another. Izzy has to look first where her fingers are going. Mom comes in. "Good, you're practicing!" she says. Izzy nods. After fifteen minutes she's had enough. And that's all she needs to do anyway. 'I wish I could already play fluently,' Izzy thinks.

At exactly 11 o' clock Nina rings the doorbell. Izzy is glad to see her again. She tells about her days with Nan. Nina went away for a couple of days as well. To a little house on the moors, with her parents and the twins. There was a swimming pool nearby. "It was really nice," says Nina. "Only Jolene and Mara were fighting a lot," she tells. "But they were short fights. Sometimes they are SO mad at each other! You'd think they'll never make up and be friends again. And shortly after, they're playing together as if nothing has happened." "I guess they forget right away," Izzy says. "Yes," Nina agrees. "That's the way it works, when you're little."

Earlier, Mom went for a nice long walk in the forest with Spike. Now she's back and calling them from the kitchen "Are the ladies ready to go?" "Yeess!" Izzy sings back. She and Nina put on their jackets and boots. They are going to the town centre by bike. First they have to collect the tickets. Mom has pre-ordered them. Then they go and have a nice sandwich, with hot chocolate of course. At the cinema, it's very crowded because of the holidays. All seats have been taken. They have good places in the back though. After many commercials, finally the screen widens. The real movie begins. It's a story about a school for witchcraft. There's a little red-haired witch who's really good at it. She's almost better than the teaching witches. There's a competition at the wizzard school. Of course, the witches are going to win. Because of the clever skills of the little red-haired witch. The wizzards don't like it. One night, they kidnap her. The wizzards lock up the little witch. But she's *so* smart. She liquifies herself. It's really thrilling. Nina and Izzy are sitting on the edge of their seats. One wizzard grabs the bottle containing the liquid witch. He wants to drink it. Izzy holds her breath. It feels like there's a knot in her stomach. She has goosebumps on her arms too. Suddenly, the boy who's seated next to her drops his bag of popcorn. Izzy looks sideways, startled by the noise. The boy ducks with his head under the seat before him. Izzy exhales. Oh, that's right. They're in the cinema. It's dark. Izzy can see some faces. The boy next to her is sitting in his chair again. With a bored look on his face. His friend is looking at his mobile phone all the time. The girl further down their row has covered her face with her hands. She's afraid to watch the movie. It's so scary. The girl's mother smiles while she's looking at the screen. Suddenly Izzy thinks, 'Everybody's seeing a different movie! And when the story is interesting, you get absorbed by it. It feels like it's happening for real. I had a knot in my stomach. Just like I had when the bad dream happened last night.'

Then she looks at the screen again. The wizzard got called away. Just in time. He has put the bottle back on the shelf. With the little witch still in it. There's witch help on the way. Fortunately.

The movie has a happy ending. The witches beat the wizzards and then the two schools decide to work together. Everybody's happy with that idea. When they're outside again, their eyes have to get used to the light. Mom, Nina and Izzy cycle home. They have a cup of tea together.

"What shall we do?" Nina asks once they've finished their tea. "Shall we go outside and jump on the trampoline?" Izzy suggests. "I don't really feel like it," says Nina. "Let's play a video game." "No." Izzy wrinkles her nose. "We've already been sitting inside all afternoon. I want to go outside." "But it's so cold," Nina says. "We can put on our coats, can't we?" Izzy shrugs. Nina pulls a face. "Still. You have a new Mario game, don't you?" "Yes," Izzy answers. "But I've played it so many times already with Nan this week." Mom gets up from her chair. She puts their cups in the dishwasher. "You'll figure it out," she says. Mom disappears upstairs. Izzy and Nina look each other in the face. "I'm definitely *not* going to play outside," Nina states. "But we'll jump ourselves warm in a minute!" Izzy says. "After three somersaults you'll want to take off your jacket!" "I don't want to," Nina persists. "And I don't feel like staying inside," Izzy says. "You always want to get your own way," Nina says. "Well, you're the same!" Izzy replies. They're both getting a bit upset now. Nina gets up. "I'm going home," she decides. "Perhaps Caitlin wants to play video games. She has Mario too, you know." "Nice friend you are," Izzy says. "You don't come here for my game console, do you?" Nina shrugs. She walked into the hallway and puts on her jacket. "Thanks!" she calls out.

"Alrighty!" Mom answers from upstairs. Then Nina pulls the frontdoor shut with a loud bang. Izzy stays behind in the kitchen. 'Stupid Nina,' she thinks. 'And that Caitlin is a weird girl too.' She walks into the garden. Spike runs after her. Izzy performs at least a hundred somersaults. She forgets all about the quarrel.

That night, Izzy practices with the guitar again. Dad shows her how to play chords once more. They have to take turns. "I guess we'll have to buy you your own guitar soon," Dad says. "It'll be much easier that way. Plus we can play together." Izzy nods eagerly. Her own guitar! She likes the idea very much. Later that night, Mom walks upstairs with her. Izzy crawls under the duvet. Suddenly she recalls what happened that afternoon. The quarrel with Nina. She tells Mom about it, what Nina said. What she said back. How they both got upset. Izzy even gets a bit upset talking about it now. "I was right, wasn't I?" Izzy asks. Mom doesn't answer. She just looks at Izzy. With a certain look in her eyes. Izzy can't really explain it. It's a loving look. But kind of ... blank. As if Mom doesn't have an opinion. Mom's eyes are a sort of mirror, Izzy thinks. For her to look into. This way, Izzy sees herself. And she starts hearing herself too. Because Mom's so quiet. Izzy can hear her own thoughts in the words she's saying.

It makes Izzy become quiet, too. For a little while. Then she says: "I see that I'm right. Because I believe what I think. Nina sees *she*'s right. Because she believes what she thinks." Mom nods her head. "So being right isn't really possible," Izzy ponders. Mom nods again. "Indeed," she says. "Do you remember when you were four year olds? You quarreled a lot then. Sometimes the whole street could hear you two screaming. You even pulled each others' hair sometimes! Nina's mother would come to take her home. And then an hour later you'd ask when Nina would come and play with you again. You never stayed cross. You simply forgot the whole fight immediately." Izzy nods. Just like Nina's sisters do now. When it's over, it's over. Now is a new moment. Grown ups can do the same, of course. Izzy lays still for a long time. With her eyes closed. Mom thinks she's asleep. So she gets up carefully and sneaks towards the door. Just when she goes to grab the doorknob, Izzy suddenly sits up straight in her bed. She calls out, "Then all fights are for nothing! And all wars too! They're just about thoughts! That's *really* stupid!" "Yes ... and a pity," Mom agrees. She returns and sits on Izzy's bed again. Then they're quiet together. For a long time.

CHAPTER 11

A Daymare

Izzy's allowed to walk home alone from school when Mom and Dad are working. School is not far away. Sometimes Nina comes home with her. That's always alright with Mom and Dad. Once in a while, Mom comes to fetch Izzy from school. With Spike. Izzy used to go to the after school activities centre when she was younger. That was quite nice. But being home is even more fun. Izzy always knocks three times on the door of Mom's practice. So Mom knows that she's home. Then Izzy has to walk Spike first. She doesn't always feel like it. Especially not when she's agreed to play with Nina. But it's her task, so it must be done. "In this house, we do everything together," Dad says. "We all three do our bit." Izzy's bit is tidying her room. And the mess she might make elsewhere in the house. Her drawing stuff and things like that. 'A clean house is a clear head,' Mom always says. And Izzy has to walk her dog, a short round. Usually it's fun. Spike is a sweet, silly dog. He is *so* happy when Izzy comes home! Today he jumps up in the air with all four paws at once. He runs circles around the kitchen table. He lies on his back so Izzy can stroke his belly. When she fetches his lead, Spike runs to the front door. Once there, he sits down like a good dog. Spike is well-trained. Izzy is always nice to him. But she's also a bit strict. That's okay, Spike likes it that way. Because then he knows exactly what to do. Walk nicely at Izzy's side. No pulling at the lead. Pooing at the dog toilet area near the park. And Spike often pees ten times during their round.

Izzy fastens his lead. 'Where shall I go?' she thinks. 'The park or the forest? Or simply around the block?' She choses the park near to where Nina lives. Perhaps they'll run into each other so they can walk the dog together. Izzy steps outside. Spike follows. Izzy sees David. He's coming home. She waves her hand and says "Hi" Suddenly Izzy knows, 'I no longer look at what David is doing. I look at who he *is*. A light, just like me, in a body. With thoughts about all kinds of things.'
She notices she doesn't really have an opinion about David anymore. Perhaps he'll tease or push her again some day. Izzy's sure she'll know what to do when that happens. Or what to say. She doesn't know now. But she will then. "Hi," David replies.

Izzy walks down the street with Spike. One more block and then she'll be in the park. The trees are still bare. But Izzy sees some little spring crocuses starting to bud already. And some other flowers she can't remember the name of. Izzy walks towards the dog's playfield. Spike is allowed to run free there. One of Spike's friends is there too. Harry is a little black dachshund. Spike and Harry run around the field together. They chase each other. Izzy thinks Harry is really cute. Especially when he's running.

His ears are flapping and his short legs are moving incredibly fast. His little butt wobbles this way and that. Harry's lady boss is sitting on the bench. Her name is Mrs Haines. Izzy knows her. Sometimes they have a chat, about school or the weather. Izzy walks over to the bench and sits down next to Mrs Haines.

"Hello Izzy!" Mrs Haines greets her. "Have you seen that there are little green buds in the trees now?" "Yes!" Izzy nods. "Spring is coming!" Mrs Haines continues, "I'm looking forward to it. I love to sit in the sun." Together they watch Spike and Harry playing. Harry is doing a somersault. He's covered with mud. It's dripping from his ears. "Another bath session for Harry this afternoon, I'm afraid," Mrs Haines laughs.

Suddenly they hear someone talking loudly. It's almost like screaming. A man comes walking towards them. 'He looks poor,' Izzy thinks. His clothes are far too big. The crotch of his trousers is hanging on his knees. His coat is covered with stains. One of his shoes has a large hole in it. 'Probably a vagabond,' Izzy thinks. "Don't pay attention to him, dear," Mrs Haines warns her. "I've seen that man before. He's not quite right." She taps with her finger on her forehead. The vagabond is talking to himself, it seems. Or he sees someone Izzy can't see. He looks very angry. The vagabond now passes the dog's playfield. He's cursing and flailing his arms. Then he sees Izzy and Mrs Haines. He looks surprised. "Hi," Izzy says. She waves her hand. "Don't say anything, love," Mrs Haines whispers. The man stands still for a second. It seems as though he wants to say something back. Then he turns around and walks away, softly talking to himself. Izzy would like to know what he's saying. And to whom. She watches the vagabond disappear around the corner.

Mrs Haines gets up. She calls Harry. "Time for your bath," she says to the little dog. Harry wags his tail. It looks like he fancies some scrubbing. "See you next time," Mrs Haines says. "Bye," Izzy replies. She sits on the bench for a little while longer. Spike is sniffing around, checking every nook and cranny of the field. He lifts up his leg everywhere. Just when Izzy is putting him back on the lead, she sees Nina and Caitlin. They're walking towards the pond. "Hey you!" Izzy cries out. The girls look around. Nina waves. "Hello there!" Izzy jogs towards them. Spike willingly jogs alongside her. "What are you doing?" Izzy asks. "The twins wanted to feed the ducks," Nina tells her. "But they were being *so* annoying. Then Caitlin and I decided to go without them. Mom wanted to get rid of this bread." Nina shows a big bag. "Did you see that creepy man just now?" Caitlin asks. Izzy nods. "As mad as a hatter," Caitlin states. "I think he's a creep. They should lock him up." Izzy shrugs her shoulders. 'Maybe Mom can help him,' she thinks. "May I help you feed the ducks?" she asks Nina. "Of course," her girlfriend says. "There's enough." Izzy takes a handful of crusts from the bag. The ducks are coming out of the pond already. They're not afraid of the girls. And they're not afraid of Spike either. Izzy has tied him to a tree. He's sitting there, patiently waiting. Izzy has a piece of bread in her hand. One brave duck snatches it from her fingers. It's a funny feeling, that beak. It doesn't hurt. Nina and Caitlin try it, too. The ducks eat out of their hands. Soon, all the bread is gone. Nina turns the bag upside down. The last crumbs fall onto the grass. Izzy unties Spike. "Do you want to join me?" she asks Nina and Caitlin. "No," says Nina. "We're going to my house to watch television." "Okay," Izzy says.

Lately she's been seeing a lot less of Nina. Since Caitlin came to live here. Izzy feels a bit jealous. It's not a nice feeling, but that's okay. She knows it's just a thought. And that it'll pass. Because everything is always changing. 'I could ask someone else to come and play with me,' Izzy thinks. "See you tomorrow, then!" she says and she walks on with Spike. The vagabond is nowhere to be seen now. 'Where would he sleep?' Izzy wonders. 'Here in the park? But it's so cold in the night!' Izzy shivers at the thought.

When she walks into her street, Izzy sees Dad's car on the driveway. He's home early. Izzy steps into the hallway. First she cleans Spike's muddy paws. There's always a special towel for him in the hall. Then she walks into the kitchen. Dad is just unpacking the groceries. "Hey Izzybusy!" he cries out, cheerfully. "Yo, Daddy!" Izzy smiles. "What are we having for dinner tonight?" "I'm making mushroom risotto," Dad replies. "Isn't that sticky rice?" Izzy wants to know. "Something like that, yes," Dad nods. "But it sounds rather yucky the way you put it." Izzy chuckles. "Would you like some tea?" she asks Dad. "Yes please," he says. Izzy puts water in the electric kettle. She waits until the light goes out. Then she carefully pours the hot water into two mugs. "What kind of tea?" she wants to know. "Green," Dad answers. Izzy choses strawberry flavour. She hangs the bags in the mugs. Dad's tea turns a light brown. Hers turns red. Izzy's looking at it. "This works just like the three popsicles!" she suddenly sees. "Huh?" Dad doesn't get it. "How do you mean?" "Well," Izzy explains. "The water is the Energy. It doesn't have a taste or smell. It's um … " she can't find the right word. "Neutral!" says Dad. Yes, that's what Izzy meant. She continues, "you always need water to make tea. It's the basis. Then you add tea leaves of your choice. That's your Thought. And we can see the result. And smell and taste it. That's Experience!" "That's quite clever," Dad laughs. "You have to tell Mom this one, so she can use it in her practice!"

Izzy's not finished yet. She says, "For you, it's different than for me. You thought 'green tea'. So you got light-coloured tea. Smelling like, well, tea. I thought 'strawberry'. That resulted in red tea. And we both see, taste and smell something different." "And you can feel it too," Dad adds. "When you put your finger into it!" "Yes," Izzy says. She rolls her eyes. "But that wouldn't be a very smart thing to do."

Mom comes in when dinner is almost ready. "That smells wonderful!" she says. She lifts the lid off the cooking pot. "Risotto! Lovely." Mom quickly sits down. Izzy has already set the table. She starts talking immediately. About her discovery. About tea and the three popsicles. "Drinking tea is life itself," says Mom. "Wonderful!" Then Izzy suddenly thinks about the vagabond in the park. She tells Mom the story. "Mrs Haines said he's not in his right mind," Izzy says. "Can't you help him?" Mom thinks a few seconds. "And where would he sleep?" Izzy continues. "It's super cold at night!" Mom nods. "He'll probably go to the shelter in town," she says. "A lot of vagabonds sleep there. Homeless is a better word, I guess. They're people without a home. The shelter gives them food, too. But you've inspired an idea for me, Izzy." "What's that?" Izzy asks. "To visit the shelter," Mom replies. "And talk with the homeless people. About the three popsicles." "Would that man understand?" Izzy wonders. "He really looked confused." Mom says: "That's precisely why I want to go! Every human being has a healthy mind. But sometimes it's hidden. Covered by a lot of thoughts. Confused thoughts. If you believe them, you seem to be confused." Izzy nods. She understands what Mom's saying. That's exactly how the vagabond looked to her.

"We all have weird thoughts sometimes," Mom said. "It doesn't matter. You don't need to do anything with them. But some people have a lot of weird thinking. And they believe their thoughts are true. They get totally lost in them. Then their world gets weird. It looks real and it all feels real too. Just like in your dream. But underneath those thoughts, nothing ever changes. There's always the Energy. It's always clear. The homeless man is Energy too. "He's a light, too!" Izzy says. Mom nods.

"In the United States, a lot of people have been helped already," she says. "By hearing about the three popsicles. Including people who were homeless or addicted. And people who were mentally ill in their head. In their thinking. And people in jails." Mom is quiet for a while. Then she says, "Yes. That's what I'm going to do. I'm going to give the shelter a call tomorrow, to ask whether I can help. It would be wonderful to do. Thank you, Izzy!"

Izzy is happy. She has the idea she has really helped the man already. It feels good. She remembers her dream. How real it seemed. But it was a nightmare. "The vagabond lives in a daymare," she says. "A real life 3D daymare!" Maybe we can wake him up," Mom smiles. The risotto is ready. Dad ladles it onto three plates. He grates some cheese over it. Izzy thinks it tastes wonderful.

CHAPTER 12

Schoolwork and Sea Waves

It's Tuesday morning. Izzy is in the classroom. Her writing exercise book lies in front of her. She has to write a full page today. 'I know how to write already,' Izzy thinks. 'Why do we have to keep practicing? To become faster? Who in the world still writes anyway? At home, we always use a tablet or a laptop.' Dad sometimes makes a shopping list. Or he writes something on his wall in the office. Izzy can do that. Mom does all her writing on the computer. Izzy doesn't know anybody who still writes letters. Even Nan sends her e-mails. 'School's just a bit old fashioned,' Izzy thinks.

She looks out of the window. The sun is shining. Izzy feels like wandering around in the woods. This afternoon, perhaps, with Spike. She wants to search for sticks and little bones and stones. Izzy makes beautiful things with them. At home, she has a large box with pieces of cloth. Felt, cotton and leather. There are balls of wool in the box, and needles and glue. All the things Izzy uses for her creations. She learned it from her Nan. "Nature is the biggest piece of art ever!" Nan always says. Izzy can see what she means. She always finds something nice in the woods. Big sticks which she paints in beautiful colours with dots and stripes. Thin twigs which Izzy curves into rings. She ties threads across them, like in a spider's web. Then she puts in little stones or tiny bones. She attaches feathers and other treasures. Izzy makes felt cones in which she puts large feathers. Izzy also makes leather pouches to keep stones in. And funny stick figures with faces and wild, woollen hair. She has a whole collection of them now. Maybe she's going to sell them at a garage sale. Maybe for charity.

Izzy's thinking about all that. The paper in front of her remains empty. Miss Marion walks past her table. "You're not making any progress, are you?" she says. Izzy doesn't even hear her. Izzy's body is in the classroom, but her head is in the woods. "Izzy!" the teacher calls out. "Huh?" Izzy looks up, startled. "You still haven't done anything!" Miss Marion points to the blank paper. "Um ... that's right," Izzy says. "I was thinking about the forest and ..." Miss Marion doesn't let her finish her sentence. "You were dreaming again," she concludes. "Time's almost up, Izzy. You'll have to take your exercise book home and do your writing there. I've really had enough of this. You're definitely not working hard enough." "But ..." Izzy starts. "No buts," the teacher says. "Finish your work at home. And do an extra page. As penalty. We have to work through this entire book this year. You're no exception to the rule."
Izzy is quiet for a moment. She looks up at Miss Marion, who seems to be very angry. Izzy thinks, 'what would she be afraid of now? That I'll never

learn how to write? That nobody wants to learn how to write anymore? And that she'll soon be out of a job? Or is she afraid that I have to become a vagabond when I grow up? Because I can't write fast enough? Poor Miss Marion. Shall I reassure her and tell her I'll be fine? Even though I haven't written today? Even if I'll never learn to write faster?'

Suddenly, Izzy has to laugh. There's nothing she can do to stop it. She pictures herself as a vagabond with an empty writing excercise book under her arm. Izzy can't stop laughing. Now Miss Marion becomes even angrier. "You go and cool off for a while," she says curtly. "In the hallway." Izzy gets up. She can't say anything. Shaking with laughter she gets out of the classroom. Once she's in the hallway, she laughs until she's crying. Her whole body is limp. Izzy sits down under the coat rack. There she calms down a bit, eventually. The school bell rings. All children come out of the classroom. Izzy slowly walks in to gather her things. "Have you finished laughing?" the teacher asks. Izzy nods. She's afraid to look Miss Marion in the eyes. Afraid that she'll start laughing again. "Tomorrow I want to see your exercise book, Izzy," the teacher says. "And tonight I'll talk to your parents."

Izzy remembers, tonight there will be a parent-teacher talk. They're going to discuss her grades. And probably her writing. Izzy puts the exercise book in her backpack. "See you later, then," she says. Because Izzy's parents always take her with them to parent-teacher talks. 'It's about you, isn't it?' Dad says. 'Then you have to know what we're discussing.' Izzy walks home.

First she greets Spike. He runs six times around the table out of pure joy. Then Izzy walks into the garage. She wants to knock on the door of Mom's practice, so Mom will know she's home. But Mom's just opening that door. "I'll walk you out," she says to her client. It's a gray-haired man wearing a business suit. 'Huh?' Izzy thinks. 'Walk him out? On a lead, just like Spike?' In her mind's eye, she sees a man in a suit with a lead around his neck. And her mother who lets him pee against a tree. Izzy giggles. But that is not what Mom meant. She simply accompanies the man to the front door. To let him out of the house.

The gentleman walks towards his car. He gets in and drives away. Izzy and Mom walk through the door to the kitchen. Izzy starts recounting what happened at school. "Mom, I have to do impositions. I was looking out of the window and then I forgot to do my work. I forgot that I was at school. My thoughts were outside, in the woods. And that's why Miss Marion just wasn't in my experience! And then she got mad at me. Because I wasn't working. And then I wondered whether she was afraid. And if so, of what. Then I saw myself as a vagabond with an empty notebook. And I had a laughter attack. I couldn't help myself, Mom. I knew Miss Marion had all these thoughts. It was just too funny." Izzy can't help but laugh again now that she's thinking about it.

"Perhaps she thought I was laughing at her. I honestly wasn't. Now I don't think it's funny anymore, though. Because I have to do a lot of writing today!" Izzy pulls a long face. "It's silly, isn't it? What does it matter how much I write? I'll only use computers anyway. I'd better learn how to type fast. That makes more sense. And I really don't feel like sitting down to write at home!" Mom nods. "I get that," she says. "Shall we take Spike for a walk together? We only went out for a short walk at midday. I feel like another, longer walk." Izzy thinks that's a good idea. She likes it when Mom goes with her. "We'll drink a cup of tea together afterwards," Mom continues. "I'm done working for today."

Mom puts on her coat. Izzy leashes Spike. Together they step out of the front door. "Shall we go to the woods?" Izzy asks. "I've been thinking about that all day." "Fine with me," Mom replies. They turn around the corner. Spike follows them.

The forest trail begins where the gardens end. Spike is allowed to run loose here. He races ahead to sniff around. And to pee, of course. Izzy immediately finds two small, straight sticks. Perfect for making stick figures. She puts them in her coat pocket. Mom snuffles the fresh air. "Lovely," she says. "I can smell spring coming." They're quiet for a while.

Izzy listens to the birds. She hears the creaking of tree branches. Every now and then, she picks something up. To put in her crafts box. "Look," Mom suddenly points. "A little skull. It's a mouse, I think." Izzy carefully picks up the white piece of bone. She looks at it from all angles. "Beautiful," she says. She can't wait to create something with it. Later on, at home. Once she will be finished with that stupid writing assignment.

After an hour they're back in again. Spike crawls into his basket. Mom and Izzy go into the kitchen. Mom puts the kettle on for a cup of tea. She cuts two thick slices of gingerbread cake. She puts butter on them. Yummy. They feast on the cake together. "I have to do my writing," Izzy sighs. "But I want to tinker with my new materials." The mouse skull is laying on the table before her. She has to clean it first. Perhaps she'll make a magic wand with it. She can also use it in a dream catcher. 'Or I may create a bracelet for it!' Izzy thinks. "Mom, shall I do my school work first, or shall I start with my crafts?" she asks. "What do you think?" Mom wants to know. "I want to create something with these, of course," Izzy replies, pointing at her treasures. Mom nods. She doesn't say anything. Then Izzy thinks out loud: "But then I'll be thinking about all the writing I still have to do all the time." "Mmm ..." Mom says. Again, there's silence.

Suddenly Izzy knows what she wants. "You know what?" she says. "I'm going to write now. I'll just pretend to be drawing. Letters are forms and figures, too. And I'm really good at drawing forms! That's what I'll do first. Maybe I'll get more ideas while I'm writing. About what I want to make. Then I'll do that afterwards."

She jumps up to get her backpack from the hallway. Izzy turns it upside down. Her lunchbox, two drinking cups, a pencilcase and the exercise book fall out. Izzy grabs the book and the pencilcase. Mom puts the rest in the dish-washer. "I have to make a few phone calls," Mom." says. "I'll be in my office She dissapears to her practice in the garage.

Izzy gets to work. She's writing, but she pretends to be drawing inside the lines. This way, writing is fun. Sort of. The letters are simply forms. Round and oblong; loops and stripes and curls. It's going to be a nice drawing. Izzy is satisfied. Never before has she written so fast. And so neatly. Miss Marion will be happy. Izzy puts the exercise book in the hallway. Next to her jacket. So she will not forget it, tonight. Perhaps she'll be a vagabond when she grows up, but at least one with a full exercise book.

'Crafts time!' Izzy thinks. She picks the mouse skull off the table. There's a tootbrush in the cupboard under the sink. Izzy uses it to scrub her forest treasures clean. She holds the tiny skull under the tap. With the toothbrush she carefully removes all the sand. Then it has to dry for a minute.

Meanwhile, Izzy cuts one of the sticks straight. She gets her crafts box from the closet. And some paint. Izzy paints the head a bright white. Then it has to dry again. Izzy's looking at it. When it's dry, she draws eyelashes with a black marker. They're long, curly eyelashes. She decides the mouse head needs hair. Red woollen hair. With glue, she cautiously sticks a few dreads on the head. It looks funny and a bit creepy, too. Then she glues the head onto a stick. Izzy searches for a piece of cloth. She finds a blue rag and uses it to make a cape. Izzy wraps it around the stick and fastens the cape with wool. It would be nice if the stick would remain standing.

'I need feet,' Izzy thinks. 'What do I have that would be suitable?' She rummages around in her box. A shell! That's it. Fortunately, she has excellent glue. It will make anything stick. Izzy puts a little drop on the stick. She presses it against the shell and holds it a few seconds. There, it's done. "I did it!" Izzy calls out. Mom's just appearing in the doorway. "Beautiful!" she says. "And a bit creepy too!" "Isn't it?" Izzy beams. "I think so too." Now they hear Dad in the hallway. And Spike's happy feet dancing on the wooden floor. Izzy runs over to Dad. She shows him her new creation. "It looks like something out of a horror movie!" he says. "You've done an excellent job." Dad starts cooking. Izzy clears away her things. Mom sets the table today.

After dinner they have to leave for school. The parent-teacher talk is at seven o' clock. Mom, Dad and Izzy arrive at school ten minutes early. The teacher is still talking with other parents. The three of them have to wait in the hall. Izzy's exercise books lays there, ready to be shown. Mom and Dad read some of the stories Izzy has written. There's a lot of them already. Her math exercise book isn't quite so full. Izzy doesn't work on it very often.

Two parents are leaving. Now it's their turn. Mom, Dad and Izzy enter the classroom. Izzy hands her writing exercise book to miss Marion. "Finished my work," she says. "Well done," the teacher nods. They go and sit at the group of tables where Miss Marion's things are. "Well, Izzy," she says, looking at her papers. "You're doing okay, but you spend way too much time dreaming." She gives Izzy a wink. "That's a good thing," Mom thinks. "Dreaming is a great way to create beautiful things." Dad nods. "I do a lot of dreaming at work," he says. "Then good ideas pop up out of nowhere." "I can't help it," Izzy adds. "Hmm ..." the teacher is silent for a while. "But you have to finish your work, Izzy," she says. Izzy nods. She gets that. "Your reading skills are good," Miss Marion continues. "The other subjects are average. You're drawing is fantastic. You know that already. But you have an F for math." Miss Marion sighs. She looks at Mom and Dad.

"Perhaps you should start thinking about remedial teaching," she suggests. Mom and Dad look at each other. "We'd rather work at Izzy's strong points," Mom says. "Can't she use a calculator? She already knows how to and it would solve the problem." "No, I'm afraid not," the teacher says. "That's against the rules. Izzy can use a memory card for multiplication tables. But no other tools. No aids. Those are not allowed at tests either." Mom nods, indicating she understands. It's quiet for a few seconds. Then mom asks, "Marion, isn't one of your pupils hearing impaired?" Izzy looks at her mother, bewildered. What on earth has *that* got to do with her math skills? "Indeed," Miss Marion says. "Kevin. He's doing very well." "How do you manage with dictations?" Mom wants to know. "Oh, I simply look at Kevin and I talk very clearly. Of course, he also has a hearing aid," the teacher explains. "That is a wonderful tool," Mom nods. Again, there's silence. Miss Marion looks a bit confused. Then she starts to laugh.

"You're right," she says. "It's a bit odd, actually. That we all have to learn the same things. But I have to stick to the rules. You know what? I'll talk to the head master about this." Mom looks happy. "That's great," she says. "You always come up with such good ideas, Marion! We really appreciate that." Dad hands over Izzy's school report to the teacher. "I guess we're done then?" he asks. "Um ... yes, I think so," Miss Marion says. They all get up. The teacher walks them to the door. The next Mom and Dad is already waiting.

Once they're outside, Dad says to Izzy: "I always failed at math. Now I have someone in the office to do the calculations for me. Remember Berry? He really likes working with numbers. He's very good at it, too. You know, Izzy, if you're a fish, you don't climb trees. If you're a kangaroo, you can't live at the bottom of the sea. Everybody should just do what they're good at. And together we can do everything." Izzy nods. "Shall we do who's home first?" she asks. Dad doesn't answer. He immediately starts to run. "You're cheating!" Izzy cries out. She runs after him, laughing. Too bad she's not a kangaroo. She would have won if she was.

At home they watch television together. Suddenly Izzy notices it's half past eight already. Bedtime. And she forgot to practice playing the guitar again. Oh, well. Tomorrow is another day. "I want to take a shower," Izzy says. "Fine," Mom nods. "I'll be up in a minute, when you're ready. Izzy takes a long, hot shower.

She gets into bed all warm and clean. Mom enters her room. "It's quite late already," she says. "Not much time left for stories." "Can you please tell me some more about the three popsicles?" Izzy begs. She knows Mom loves to talk about them. And Izzy doesn't feel like sleeping yet. Mom sits down on her bed. "Alright," she says. "I'll explain them in a different way."

"Do you remember when we were in France last year?" Mom asks. "Where there were such big waves in the sea?" Izzy nods. "Well," Mom continues. "you can see those waves as our own thinking. Little thoughts. Sometimes there are a lot of waves. The sea looks wild. You can see and feel it. Better not to swim in that case. The waves could pull you under water. Not a nice experience. There's a red flag at the beach to warn you." Izzy nods again.

"In the same way, you can have a lot of thoughts sometimes," Mom says. "Troubled thoughts." "Like the vagabond!" Izzy says. "Exactly," Mom says. "And it's better not to do anything in that case." Izzy gets that. A red flag means no swimming. Troubled thoughts mean no action.

Mom continues. "Another time, the sea is calm," she says. "The waves come one by one. You can easily float on them. When there's a green flag at the beach, you're allowed to swim. In the same way, when your head is calm, you can just do what occurs to you." Izzy is quiet for a while. "I'm still missing a popsicle!" she says. Where's the Energy in this story?"

"Ah very good!" Mom says. "That's the sea itself. Beneath all those waves, there's the stillness of the deep sea. You can't see it. But you can feel it if you dive down through the waves. It's awfully quiet and yet ... very alive. That's where the big currents are. Big thinking. The Energy.

You can also look at it this way, we are all little waves. You, me, Dad and Nan, other Nan and Grandpa, Rose and Max. Nina, Miss Marion and everybody. Waves with our own thoughts. Our own little stories. But we're also part of the sea. That's the Energy that gives us life and moves us." "Hmmm ..." Izzy murmurs.

"The funny thing is," Mom says, "that you often can't see the sea when you're a little wave. Do you know why? Because the sea is everywhere around you. Because you're in it. Because you *are* it!" Izzy pictures a big ocean. With a lot of different waves. People don't know that they're the sea, too. It looks so funny. "That's why you and Dad have a waterbed" she laughs. "Of course, to remember and feel that you're a wave in the sea all night!" Mom laughs with her. "Yes, smarty pants," she says, "and now I'm going to float downstairs. Sleep well." "Good night, Mom," Izzy says "Beware of flooding - and don't get seasick!" She hears Mom laughing all the way down the stairs.

CHAPTER 13

Izzy Takes the Elevator

Izzy has to give a speech in school. In Primary 4 it was optional, you didn't have to. Now it's compulsory. She paid attention when her classmates did a speech so she sort of knows how it works. Fifteen minutes in front of the classroom, alone. Izzy doesn't like the idea at all. She's a bit scared to stand there with everybody looking at her. Now it's Saturday. Only two days to go before her speech on Monday. "I guess I have to start preparations," Izzy's thinking. She's with Mom and Dad in the car. They're on their way to see Aunt Wendy, Mom's youngest sister, to have a cup of coffee and cake. They like to hang out together.

"What subject shall I talk about in my speech?" Izzy asks. Dad shrugs his shoulders. "What do you want to talk about?" he asks. "I really don't know," Izzy sighs. Mom remains silent. The radio is on. A girl is singing a beautiful song and playing the guitar. "Perhaps about guitar playing," Izzy says. Dad likes the idea immediately. "Yes! You could take my guitar to school," he suggests. "And play a little song!" "I'm not good enough yet," Izzy replies. "And I don't dare. So that's not an option. I've started much too late anyway. I ought to go to the library to pick up some books. But it's not open until

Monday. And my speech is on Monday already!" "I'm sure you'll find a subject," Mom reassures her. They park the car in front of Wendy's appartment building.

Izzy runs ahead of Mom and Dad and is the first to get inside. She loves taking the elevator up! She waits for Mom and Dad to come in and then pushes the right button. The elevator doors close and they whizz up to the fifteenth floor. Wendy is already waiting for them in the hall. Izzy thinks she's really beautiful. Wendy has long blonde hair and brown eyes. She is much taller than Mom. 'I've had more kicks in the butt,' Wendy always says. But that's just a joke. Izzy gives her a big hug. Wendy's cats are snoozing and don't even bother to look up when they enter. They don't go all crazy when someone comes in, like Spike does.

Bill and Vera are special cats. Long-haired Persians, Izzy has learned. They're a beautiful red colour. Wendy has to comb them every single day. Otherwise their fur gets all tangled. Izzy pets Bill who's laying in the window sill. He feels nice and soft. Especially behind his ears. Izzy looks out of the big window. It's quite cloudy. Still, Izzy can see a very long way. She sees almost the entire town. With a lot of little cars and little people scurrying around. Izzy sees the big church as well. She stands there staring at it for some time. She's tickling Bill on his head and he's purring sofly. Suddenly Izzy thinks, 'I can talk about Bill and

Vera! Wendy has books with all the information on their breed. She will definitely allow me to borrow them. And Wendy probably has pictures of them, too.'

Mom and Dad are sitting at Wendy's dining table. Wendy's making coffee. "What would you like to drink, Izzy?" she calls out from the kitchen. "Water, please," Izzy replies. She walks into the kitchen. "Wendy, can I borrow your books about the cats?" Izzy asks. "I want to do a speech about their breed." "Of course!" Wendy says. "And do you have any pictures of them?" "Sure," Wendy nods. "When do you have to do the speech?" "Monday" Izzy says gloomily. "At what time?" Wendy asks. "After lunch break," Izzy answers. "At half past one." "Well," Wendy laughs, "what a coincidence! I have to take Bill and Vera to the vet on Monday. They'll get a shot at two o'clock. The vet is close to your school. Shall I drop by with them on my way? Then your classmates can see Bill and Vera." "Yes!" Izzy cheers. "That'll be fun! And it shortens my talking time when I have something to show. I won't need to remember so many lines!" "Then let's do it," Wendy laughs.

Izzy hops over to the bookcase. She finds five books on Persian cats. Izzy selects the two thinnest. Then it's time for a slice of pear cake. Wendy has baked one herself. It tastes lovely. Mom, Dad and Wendy are chatting while Izzy flips through the booklets. There are a lot of difficult words in them. But Izzy doesn't worry about that. She can look them up at the computer at home. And Google knows a lot about cats, too.

On Sunday, Izzy's working on her speech. She uses the computer and Internet. Izzy finds a couple of sites about long-haired Persians. It says where they originally come from. Why they're called Persians, what they like to eat and why people have cats. She finds a piece of text about their flat noses. And also something about how to take care of their fur. Izzy cuts and pastes some sentences. She writes a few herself. She picks some information out of the booklets. She'll take those with her to school as well. She doesn't really need pictures, as she can simply show Bill and Vera! Well, perhaps a picture of Persians with different colours. Bill and Vera are both red. But there are also white Persians, and grey ones and brown. And multi-coloured Persians, too. 'There you go,' Izzy thinks. 'That's another three sentences.' Tomorrow, at the end of the lunch break, Wendy will bring the cats to school in their travel baskets. Then Wendy will wait in the hallway. Or maybe she's allowed to stay and sit in the classroom, so she can listen to Izzy's speech. Afterwards, Wendy will take Bill and Vera to the vet. That's how they've planned it. Izzy only needs to learn a couple of sentences by heart. She's not really good at that. She keeps forgetting the words.

When her speech is ready, Izzy wants to practice. Dad will play the audience. Spike needs to pretend he's a cat, so Izzy can use him to show her listeners. "This kind of hair needs to be brushed every day," Izzy points to Spike. He looks up at her, puzzled. Mom only brushes him once a week! He needs to have a daily brush session too! Do you have to be a cat for that, or what? "If I tickle Bill behind his ears, he will start to purr," Izzy continues. "Listen." She tickles Spike behind his right ear. He doesn't purr. "You must be a bit more co-operative, Spike," Izzy laughs. "You're a bad actor." Spike doesn't get it at all. He wants to go and lie in his basket. He's tired after the long walk they took that morning. Dad applauds. "Wonderful speech!" he says. "Only the cat has to be retrained. He's not acting like a cat at all." They laugh out loud. Spike crawls into his basket, with an indignant expression on his face. 'Weird people,' Izzy sees him thinking.

That evening, Mom walks upstairs with Izzy. By now, Izzy has the speech in her head. At least, sort of. "But I bet I won't remember anything tomorrow" she sighs. "Why do I have to do this? Speeches are stupid." It's silent for a while. Mom strokes Izzy's hair. "I just won't think about it anymore," Izzy decides. "That seems to be a good idea," Mom begins. "But will it work? I sometimes have things I don't want to think about. And then I can't think of anything else! If I say to you, *don't* think about a yellow dotted rhino and a red striped bear on a seesaw. Then that's exactly the image that will come into your head." Izzy nods. She can see the picture already. Mom continues, "*never* before did you think about a yellow dotted rhino and a red striped bear on a seesaw. Until I told you not to think about them." "True," Izzy says. "But then what should I do? Tomorrow is the speech. I'm scared that it doesn't go well. That they'll laugh at me. That I'll get an F and that everybody will think I'm dumb. I don't want to think about that. Otherwise I can't sleep. And it doesn't feel good."

"Hmm ..." Mom says. "That's a lot of scared thoughts indeed. I understand you feel frightened. Are there any children who actually like to give speeches?" "Um ... yes!" Izzy replies. "Julius! He's done two speeches this year. And last year he did one as well, even when it wasn't compulsory!" Again, it's quiet for a little while. Mom is rubbing Izzy's feet warm. Suddenly Izzy sits up straight and calls out: "The 'stupid' isn't about the speech, is it? It's in my thinking about the speech. It's inside-out!" Mom nods. "The three popsicles again," Izzy murmurs.

"The speech doesn't scare me. Speeches don't do anything. I feel scared because I have these thoughts! Or rather, because I *believe* those thoughts. Julius has different thinking about speeches. He loves to do them. So he doesn't feel any fear." Mom nods. "Brilliant," she says. "Are your feet nice and warm now?" They are. Mom gets up. "Sleep well, honey," she says. Izzy gets a kiss on the forehead and one on her nose. Then Mom goes downstairs.

'What a comfy bed I have,' Izzy thinks. She crawls deep under the duvet. Now and then a thought pops into her head about the speech. But Izzy knows she doesn't have to believe it. She smiles and falls asleep soon after.

The next morning Izzy's reading her speech one more time during breakfast. Dad has made her a smoothie with avocado. It tastes wonderful. Izzy is slowly sipping from her cup. Then she puts all the items she needs for her speech into her back pack. "Are you ready to go and do it?" Dad asks. Izzy shrugs her shoulders. "I guess so." She turns to her mother and says, "I'm going to leave those frightful thoughts at home, Mom! So I'll have more space in my head for the words of my speech." "That's fine," Mom nods with a serious look on her face. "I'll take good care of them. What do you usually feed them? I'll make sure they'll get it now!" Izzy laughs.

"Good luck," Dad says while he gets up to go to work. "And say hello to Bill and Vera and Wendy!" Izzy nods. She can't say anything because her mouth is full of toothpaste. The doorbell rings. Nina is here. Izzy quickly rinses her mouth. Dad has opened the door already. "Are you coming?" Nina asks. "Yes!" says Izzy. Mom gets a kiss. "Have fun," she says. Then Izzy and Nina step outside. They haven't seen each other this past weekend. Nina tells Izzy that she went swimming and Izzy tells Nina about her weekend. Soon they're at school.

At the end of the lunch break, Izzy spots Wendy. She's just getting the cats' baskets out of her car. Izzy runs towards her aunt. She takes Wendy and the cats inside, to her classroom. Together they do the preparations. They lay the booklets on the teacher's table with a piece of paper on which Izzy has written a few words. And the cat baskets, of course. Bill and Vera are looking out curiously. Bill tries to stick his little nose through the bars. He's never been in school before! Miss Marion enters the classroom. She shakes hands with Wendy. "I don't mind if you stay," she says. "There's an empty seat in the back of the classroom for you." "I'd like that," Wendy replies. Now all the children come in. They're all curious about the cat baskets. Izzy feels a flutter in her stomach. She takes a deep breath. When everybody has taken their seat, Miss Marion nods. Izzy can begin. Only, she doesn't know how. What was her opening line again? The flutter turns into a knot. Children are shuffling their feet. Izzy looks at Wendy, who gives her an encouraging smile and a nod. 'You can do it,' her eyes are saying. Izzy slowly breathes in and out. Her mind is blank.

Then suddenly it occurs to her to get Vera out. And that's what she does. Izzy opens Vera's basket and takes out the cat. She puts Vera on her lap and sits down on the teacher's table. Izzy holds the cat carefully but firmly. The way Wendy taught her.

"This is Vera," Izzy begins. "She's a long-haired Persian. I would like to tell you some things about this breed." Then the words come out effortlessly. Izzy tells everything she knows about long-haired Persians. She knows even more than she thought she did! Izzy even tells some things that are not on her paper! After a while, she's done. Izzy tickles Vera behind her ear. Vera makes a purring sound. "Vera is satisfied with everything I said about her," Izzy laughs. "If you listen closely, you can hear her purring." The class is silent. The only sound is Vera's purring. "That was my speech," Izzy solemnly concludes. "I want to thank Vera for her kind co-operation." The children softly clap their hands. They don't want to scare Bill and Vera. "Well done, Izzy," the teacher says. Wendy walks to the front of the classroom to put Vera back in her basket.
"You were amazing!" Wendy whispers in Izzy's ear. She leaves for the vet with the cats. Izzy happily sits down in her seat. 'That wasn't too bad,' she thinks.

Mom comes to fetch her from school with Spike. Izzy runs towards her, together with Nina. "How did the speech go?" Mom asks. "Very well," Izzy says. "It was kind of weird. In the beginning, I couldn't remember anything. It was like I wasn't able to access the right words. As if I couldn't see them. Just like when you're at the ground floor at Wendy's appartment building. You know the entire town is surrounding it. But you can't see it. I just stayed quiet for a few seconds. Then it seemed as though I automatically took the elevator. It went all the way up. There I could see everything, the whole town. Suddenly I decided to take Vera out and all the right words just came out. The words were there already, I only had to go to the top floor where I could see them." "That's a beautiful comparison," Mom thinks. "I'm glad it went well. A hot chocolate with cream to celebrate, I suppose? "Yes!" Izzy cheers. "Can Nina come with us?" "Of course," Mom replies. The three of them walk home. Spike is frolicking at Izzy's side. He's happy too. Although he doesn't know why. Dogs don't think that much. That helps.

CHAPTER 14

What is True?

That night in bed Izzy asks Mom, "Why does thinking exist anyway? It's only bothering us!" "Well, I see it as a gift," Mom says. "Hmm," Izzy mutters, "it wasn't on my wishlist for Christmas. Or my birthday." "If there was no Thought," Mom explains "you wouldn't have an experience. So there wouldn't be a Spike. There wouldn't be a Nina and there wouldn't be hot chocolate. There wouldn't be any drawings, music, stars and no Mom ... You wouldn't know what it all was. Whatever you would see and hear and feel and smell and taste would be the same. Everything would be one." Izzy thinks for a while. "But surely I don't need a thought to see Spike?" she asks. "Perhaps I should explain it in a different way," Mom says. "Everything you know is thought too. When you're born, you're like an empty computer. Without programs. Or like a blank sheet of paper. Babies are a piece of pure Energy in the form of a tiny body." "So they *do* have the big thinking!" Izzy says. "There's nothing in their computer yet, but they're already on-line!" Mom nods in agreement. "Exactly!" she smiles. "You're born with everything you'll ever need. And then you add to that, all kinds of things that you learn. Things that serve you. Like what a dog is. How to ask for food. That a stove can be hot. But you also learn things that don't serve you. That you can do something the wrong way, for instance. Or that you have to be scared of something. People tell you, or you just feel it. You pick it up from everyone around you. Because they all think the same way, more or less. Then you start to think like them. That's normal. And there's different thinking everywhere in the world. When you're born in a little village in Africa you learn different things than when you're born here.

"Hmmm ..." Izzy ponders. "So if I knew nothing about you and I didn't have any thoughts about you, I wouldn't know you?" Mom laughs. She says:" Well, actually, you don't really know anybody. You only know what you think about somebody. You only know the story in your head. And that's not who someone *is*. For example, sometimes you may think I'm a silly mother. Sometimes you may think I'm the best mom in the world. I haven't changed, but your thoughts have. Perhaps you were in a bad mood one time. The other time you were in a good mood."

Izzy looks at Mom with eyes as big as saucers. "Then that's true the other way around too!" she calls out. "When you're cross with me! You're simply in a grumpy mood, so you have grumpy thoughts. And then you think it's my fault! You think it's because of something I'm doing!" "That's right," Mom says. "Because sometimes," Izzy continues, "I'm singing loud and you join me. But

109

another time you ask me if I could please stop the noise!" "Well, that's just because you're singing off-key," Mom teases her. "But you're right. That's true." "So if you're angry, I don't need to listen to you," Izzy states. "No," Mom says, laughing. "if I were you, I would hide myself until my foul mood is gone." "I will," Izzy says. "Or I'll call out, 'Your thoughts are fooling you!'"
"Exactly!" Mom nods. "Of course, sometimes we have different ideas about something. About cleaning up your room, for instance. How often you should do that. And maybe about what 'clean' is. So we have to discuss that. I usually wait until we're both in a good mood. Until our lights are both green, so to speak. Then we can solve things easily. Without fighting." Izzy thinks 'That's right, that's the way Mom does it.'

"But what about bullying, for example" Izzy says. "That's stupid." Mom nods. "So, you have to learn that you can't do that," Izzy continues. "Because otherwise you don't know it's an awful thing to do." "Mmm ..." Mom ponders. "What if every child knew we're all the same light. And every child knew they had to pay attention to his or her feelings. To their warning signal. Then everybody would know that they should not act when their warning signal is red. When they don't feel good." Izzy thinks about these words. Then she slowly says: "I guess ... in that case, nobody would bully anyone. Because when you feel good, you don't bully." "That's right," Mom agrees. "When you feel good, you're nice to yourself and to others. You don't bully and you won't start a fight."

Izzy sort of gets that, but still has a question: "If it's all just our thinking, then what is true?" "That's a wonderful question," Mom says. "And there isn't really a right answer. It's a big mystery, really, those three popsicles.

Sometimes, when I'm very quiet in my head, I can feel the Energy. I know things. But as soon as I start thinking about it, it's not true anymore. Because I'm using my thinking. When I talk about it, it's just words. So it can't really be explained. What's true can't be seen, can't be touched, can't be smelled or heard. I can try to explain to you how I think it works, but still, that's not really it. What's true, you'll have to experience for yourself. And that's something everybody can do, because everybody is the Energy, the three popsicles in action."

That went over Izzy's head. But that's no problem, because she doesn't need to think about all this. It's no use anyway. She knows her thinking would only get more confused if she did.

However, another question comes into her mind and Izzy asks, "All those people who come to you, they all have problems, don't they?" Mom smiles. "They usually think they do, yes!" "And then you tell them what to do, right?" Izzy guesses. "No,"

Mom says, "they know what to do or what not to do themselves." "Huh?" Izzy is surprised. "But then why do they come to you?" "Because they don't know that they know. They don't remember who they really are." "Oh," Izzy says. She's quiet for a minute. Then she jumps up. "I get it! You tell them about the popsicles and then they see it for themselves!" "Yes," Mom nods. "That's it. The beautiful thing is, that when they know, they can always see solutions for themselves. Or rather, they don't see the problems anymore. So they don't have to come back to me. Because every problem is in their own thinking." "Luckily, new people come all the time," Izzy chuckles. Mom likes that idea, too. She loves talking about the three popsicles. "Now it's time to go to sleep," Mom decides. "I'm going to take a look in my book of drawings," Izzy says. "All right," Mom replies and she gives Izzy a big kiss. Then she disappears downstairs.

The next day, Izzy has a guitar lesson. She almost forgot, like she keeps forgetting to practice. This week she's picked up dad's guitar only twice. 'Oh, well. I'm going to pay attention in class,' Izzy thinks. Nina walks with her that afternoon. "I've asked my parents if I could have guitar lessons, too," Nina tells her. "But my dad said it's too expensive. Because I already have jazz ballet lessons and gymnastics practice." "That's too bad," Izzy thinks. They spot David who's also going to the guitar lesson. He's carrying a guitar case. "I'm glad I don't need to spend time with David every week, though,"

Nina says. "He's always acting really stupid!" "He's not too bad, you know," Izzy reckons. They overtake David. "Hi," Izzy says. "I have my own guitar!" David points at the case. "This is much better, my father says so." "Cool!" Izzy nods. "Will you get your own guitar?" David asks. "I don't know," Izzy replies. "Maybe."

David says: "I haven't practiced at all this week. I already know how to play." "That's nice," Izzy says. She knows it's probably not true. She senses that David wants to show off. That's okay. 'He's just scared to not be seen as cool,' Izzy thinks. "I've played twice," she says. "But it didn't go very well." She looks straight into David's eyes. He's quiet for a second. "I'm sure you'll learn, too," David eventually states. Nina looks surprised. She's never heard David talk this way before.

The guitar lesson is fun. They're allowed to improvise for a change. Just do whatever occurs to you. That's the way Izzy likes best. If she's not paying attention, she even plays the chords a lot smoother. 'Maybe I should quit these lessons,' Izzy thinks. 'And simply improvise on Dad's guitar.' She decides she's going to discuss it with Mom and Dad later on. The hour passes quite quickly. Izzy walks home with David. He acts normal. Almost nice.
At home, Izzy sees Dad's car parked on the driveway already. The front door opens. Spike dashes outside. Nan walks behind him with her arms wide open. "Isabella!" she calls out. "There

you are!" "Nan! What a surprise!" Izzy laughs. She wraps her arms around Nan. "You're quite late from school, dear," Nan says. "Do they have to keep you that long? There should be a law against it!" Izzy chuckles. "No Nan, I had to go to my guitar lesson." "Ah!" Nan exclaims. "That reminds me. Dad and I have a surprise for you." Now Izzy gets curious. "What is it?" she asks. "We're going to have a cup of tea first," Nan decides. "With muffins from the gourmet bakery shop." "Nice!" says Izzy. She skips inside. There's Dad.

"Nan has worked with me at the office today," Dad tells her. "She has been testing our new computer game." "And discovered some errors!" Nan exclaims. "That too, yes," Dad admits. "I've got a sore thumb now," Nan says. "But the game is fantastic! I want to have it as soon as it's released!" Meanwhile, Dad has made a cup of tea for them. "Deal," he nods, "you'll get the very first one. And Izzy, Nan and I have bought you something in town. A present." "Where is it?" Izzy wants to know. Nan ducks under the table. She produces a big packet. Nan hands it over to Izzy. "This is for you, Isabella," she says solemnly. "I hope you'll have a lot of fun playing it."

Izzy immediately sees what it is. Nan and Dad have bought her a guitar. Just now that she wants to stop taking lessons. For a second, she doesn't know what to say. "Don't you want it?" Nan asks. "Um ... of course I do! Yes!" Izzy stammers. Her face becomes a bright red. She tears the paper off the packet. "It's absolutely perfect." She caresses the wood. It's smooth and shiny. The guitar is neatly stringed and ready to play. So that's what Izzy does. It sounds wonderful. "Thank you so much, Nan!" she says and gives her Nan a hug. "What about me?" Dad begs. "You too!" Izzy calls out and plants a big kiss on his cheek. "Now we can practice together," Dad says, pleased. Izzy nods. "Today we were allowed to improvise. That's the way I like to play best." "Indeed," Dad agrees. "And if you know the basics, it becomes even better." They drink their tea. The muffins Nan brought with her taste fabulous. "I can't eat dinner," Izzy sighs when she has devoured two of them. "I'll have a cheap night then!" Dad laughs. "We're going out for dinner with Nan later. When mom gets home." Mom is working at the homeless shelter this afternoon. She goes there every week now for a couple of hours. Mom likes it very much. She has good conversations with the homeless. About the three popsicles.

Dinner with Nan is fun. Afterwards, they take her home. Mom and Dad have a cup of coffee at Nan's place. Therefore they're home quite late. Izzy should have been in bed already. "I'm going to take a shower," she says. "Fine," Mom says. "I'll come up to give you a goodnight kiss later." In the shower, Izzy thinks about the guitar again. It was probably very expensive. Now she can't say that she wants to quit the lessons anymore. It would be such a waste of money. The lessons were expensive too, Nina said. And Dad enjoys practicing together so much.

And Nan hopes she'll get really good at it and play in a band. Just like her dad used to do. Izzy utters a deep sigh. She doesn't want to disappoint anyone. She doesn't know what to do now. Stick with it anyway? Perhaps Nina can take her place in the lessons? No, Mom and Dad have paid for it. And then still, there's the guitar. And everything everybody's expecting from her. Perhaps she should just practice more often. But she doesn't feel like practicing at all. Izzy sighs again. She turns off the tap. She hasn't even felt the warm water. She was too busy with everything that was going on in her head. 'I'm in deep trouble,' Izzy thinks. "Hey, that was an awful thought!" she says out loud. No wonder she feels bad. And all the while she's simply standing in the bathroom. Where nothing's going on. "And I don't even know whether it's all true!" Izzy calls out.

Mom pops her head around the door. "Whether what's true?" she asks, nonplussed. "Are you ready? You've been in the shower for over twenty minutes." "I was worrying," Izzy laughs. "That takes a lot of time." Mom has to laugh, too. "That's right," she nods. "Is there anything I can help you with?" "Nope." Izzy shakes her head. "I'm going to bed now. Mom tucks her in with a big kiss. Just before she falls asleep, Izzy hears a soft little voice inside her head. 'Improvise,' the little voice says. Izzy is asleep already. All the thoughts have vanished from her head.

The alarm goes off. Izzy wakes up. The soft little voice is there immediately. 'Improvise,' it says. Izzy jumps out of bed and puts her clothes on. Then she walks downstairs. Mom is in the kitchen. Dad has left early today. Izzy says: "Big thinking is a soft voice in the silence. Little thinking is loud voices making a racket." "And a good morning to you too!" Mom laughs. "What wisdom at this early hour!" Izzy nods. "Yesterday, I was worrying about the guitar lessons," she says. "Or rather, about the money for the guitar lessons and the guitar. Because I don't really enjoy it. And I wanted to quit. I was scared that you would be angry. And I was worried about what Nan would think. And about what Dad would think. And about what you would think. But I have no clue what you're thinking. That's only my thinking. About what you're all thinking. It doesn't need to be true!" Mom nods. "I'm surprised you didn't spend three hours in the shower! With all that thinking going on!" Izzy chuckles.

She continues: "Then I lay still in bed. And heard a little voice. I guess it was the Energy. I heard 'improvise'. I really like that. To be free to play whatever I want. So I was thinking; what about if I take lessons until summer break? And then quit, but play the guitar when and in the way I want?" "Of course," Mom replies. You don't have to do anything ... and Izzy, if we spend money on you, then that's our choice. You don't need to be concerned about that." Izzy is happy. 'Mom gets it.'

Izzy's looking forward to playing the guitar this afternoon. Improvising a bit.

CHAPTER 15

Izzy Vacuums a Song

Today is Saturday. Izzy and Nina have been playing in the woods this morning. They took Spike with them and had a lot of fun together. Now Izzy's back home. Nina had to leave. She was going with her parents to visit her grandparents. Dad's in the kitchen. He's preparing lunch. He's made soup. Mom is still talking with a client. They come on Saturdays sometimes, to learn about the three popsicles. Izzy can hear the client leave now. There's laughter in the garage.

Mom enters and sticks her nose in the kitchen, smelling the yummy smells. "Minestrone!" she calls out. "I love it!" "Please be seated, madam," Dad says, sounding very posh. "The soup will be served in a minute," Izzy has neatly folded paper napkins and put them on the plates. "It feels like being out for dinner again," Mom says. "Very elegant." They enjoy their soup. There's bread from the oven as well, with garlic and tomato. Mom asks Izzy: "Are you going with us to Karen this afternoon?" Karen is one of their neighbours. "Her baby has just been born. It's a boy! His name is Ian." "That's right" replies Izzy. "I saw their birth announcement card the other day." "They're having a party today," Mom says. "To celebrate Ian's birth. It starts at three o'clock. You can come if you want." "Sure, it sounds fun," Izzy nods. There will probably be more children.

"Have you tidied your room already?" Mom asks. That's Izzy's weekly chore on Saturday. "No," Izzy answers. "I've been playing with Nina. We went to the woods and took Spike." "You'd better start immediately after lunch," Mom suggests. "I want to vacuum upstairs before we leave for the party." Izzy nods. When she has finished her soup, she runs upstairs to her room. It's quite a mess. Clothes lay strewn everywhere. And cuddly toys she played with. And playing cards that have been there for days already. She tried to do some tricks with Nina. The twister mat has been left out and Izzy spots a drafting compass on the floor. She picks it up and brings it to her little desk. There's a stack of paper there. Izzy sits down on her chair. She draws a couple of circles with the drafting compass. Big ones and small ones. They look like bubbles. Perhaps she can draw a girl who's blowing bubbles. And in the bubbles she can draw the images the girl is seeing. Soon Izzy is absorbed in her drawing. Then Mom enters. "Izzy!" she calls out. "Your room is still a big mess! You promised to tidy up! I can't vacuum this way, can I?" Mom looks cross. Her voice sounds angry as well. "Sorry, Mom," Izzy says. "I'm starting right now, okay?" "I want to leave for the party in forty minutes," Mom continues to grumble. "And I need to shower before we go." "You know what?" Izzy says. "Go and have a shower now.

I'll tidy up in the meantime. And I'll vacuum my room myself, later today, or tomorrow." Mom disappears from her room. Izzy starts picking up her stuff.

After half an hour, all of it is gone. Mom is ready too. They meet in the hallway. "Sorry for getting cross with you, Izzy," Mom says. "That wasn't necessary. We do have an agreement about doing your chores on time. If you can't manage, I'd like to know. So we can work out together where things go wrong. And how you can do it differently." Izzy nods. "I can manage," she says. "I just sat down to draw something. And then I forgot all about the mess." "Yes, that's the way it goes sometimes," Mom smiles. "And this was a great example of how it works with the popsicles. I had a schedule in my head. It seemed to be very important. I wanted to do everything on time. When that didn't work out, I got angry. And I thought you and your mess were the cause. But the real reason was my thinking. Because suppose a fire broke out. In that case, I wouldn't care if there were a mess in your room. My schedule wouldn't be important at all. Isn't that funny? It's just what we're thinking what's important in the moment. And that changes all the time!" Izzy gets that. Mom con-tinues: "Nothing is important in and of itself. You decide what's important for you," she says. "Except for a tidy room, of course. That's *always very, very* important!" Mom makes a funny angry face. Izzy can tell she's joking and laughs. She prefers a tidy and clean room herself, most of the time.

"Sooooo …" Izzy says. "When I'm cross it's always my own problem?" "It's not a problem at all," Mom laughs. "You simply have angry thoughts about someone or something. Just like I had about you and the cleaning up. You believe those thoughts. They give you an angry feeling and you blame someone else for that. That's all." Izzy looks surprised. "That's really turning around everything," she says with big eyes "Yes," Mom nods. "It's knowing that we live from the inside out." She looks into Izzy's room. "Neat," Mom says. "Let's go to Karen's and see little Ian."

They walk down the street. Dad will join them later. He's taking Spike for a little walk first. It's clear where the party is. The house is decorated with a host of balloons, in all the colours of the rainbow. Izzy gives Karen a present for her baby son. It's a tiny pair of jeans. Dad bought them the other day. Karen loves the present. Ian has no opinion yet. He's asleep in his crib in a corner of the room. There's a long table with food and drinks. Cake, crisps, lemonade, fruit skewers, cheese and toast. Ian doesn't get to taste any of it. 'Babies only drink milk,' Izzy thinks to herself. She walks towards Ian. He's just waking up. Izzy looks into his eyes. They're like big, blue marbles. Ian stares back. They're both quiet. Then Ian wrinkles his little nose and makes a weird sound. He looks at Izzy, startled by his own voice. It's funny to see. Mom is standing next to her now. She's looking at Ian, too. "Isn't he sweet?" she says. Izzy nods. "Just now, it looked like he was startled by his own voice!" she says. "Yes, that happens sometimes," Mom says. "Or they are surprised by their own hand passing in front of their eyes. Babies don't know that hand belongs to them. They still have a lot to discover." That makes Izzy laugh. "Being scared by your own voice," she giggles. "Now that's funny! Imagine me screaming at myself: 'IZZY!! I'M GOING TO GET YOU!!' And then getting scared and running away!" Izzy can totally see the picture. "No," Mom chuckles. "That's impossible. When you're older, you can only scare yourself with your own thoughts." Izzy points at Ian, "He doesn't have any thoughts yet. He doesn't know anything. Still, he seems to be wise. There are no clouds covering his light yet." "Yes," Mom says. "Did you notice? That's why people love to look at babies. They're so pure." "You stay like this," Izzy whispers into Ian's tiny ear. "Without little thinking. That's so much easier." Mom laughs. "I don't think that's possible," she says. "You only think that!" Izzy giggles. She caresses Ian's chubby arm. "Is he only seeing and feeling Energy?" she asks Mom. "Because he has no names for anything yet?" Mom hesitates. "Well, perhaps he is. Because he still so young. But I'm not sure. What do you think?" Izzy can't remember how it felt to be a baby. "Small children are very wise," Mom says. "They often know things nobody told them." "Was I like that?" "Definitely," Mom replies. "You had very original ideas."

More people come in to see little Ian. Karen gets the baby out of his crib. "Hi Izzy," another neighbour greets her. It's David's mother. "How are you?" "Very well!" Izzy replies. "And how about school?" David's mom asks. Izzy shrugs her shoulders. "Not too bad, I guess. Except for maths. But I don't worry about it anymore and then I get better grades. Because I know more when I'm on-line." David's mom looks puzzled. She has no clue what Izzy's talking about. Izzy quickly thinks of something else to say. "I'm in the same group as David at guitar lessons," she mentions. David's mom smiles proudly. "So David told me, dear. He plays quite well, doesn't he? He practices every day!" "Good for him," Izzy says. "I can't make myself do that." Then she feels like a bite. "I'm going to eat something," she tells David's mom, who nods and says: "I'll talk to you later, Izzy."

Izzy walks toward the long table with food. There's so much to choose from! She hardly knows what to take. Izzy's mouth is watering when she looks at the cakes and crisps. 'That's so funny,' Izzy thinks. 'I only think about food and my mouth produces spit already!' She takes a plate and chooses a piece of cake. It's delicious.

After an hour, Izzy gets bored. There aren't as many children at the party as she had hoped. She walks up to Dad. He's talking with one of the neighbours and having a good time. "I think I'm going home now," Izzy says. "Sure," Dad nods. "Have you got a key?" She hasn't, so Dad gives her his own key. "Just leave the door of the garage open," Dad tells her. Izzy says goodbye to her Mom and Karen and her husband and walks home. 'What shall I do now?' Izzy wonders. She doesn't know yet. She decides to vacuum her room first because she promised Mom she would. Izzy walks upstairs. Vacuuming is kind of fun. She creates nice striping patterns in the carpet. Izzy isn't thinking about anything. Her head is empty. Just like baby Ian's. There's only the sound of the vacuum cleaner. It's an old one. It creaks and pops and wheezes and makes a lot of noise. Izzy hears a tune in the noise. The vacuum cleaner is singing! Izzy closely listens to the creaking song.

When she's finished, she puts the vacuum cleaner in the hallway, where Mom can find it later on and put it away. Then Izzy walks downstairs. In the living room she picks up her guitar. Izzy starts playing the vaccum cleaner's song. The words simply pop into her mind. Izzy sings:

Don't worry, don't you worry
There's no need to hurry
A light shines bright inside of me
Although surely, I can't always see
But when I feel a red light blinking
I know it's just my thinking

Three popsicles, three popsicles
All you need to know
I'm living from the inside out
I'm going with the flow

When I don't feel very nice
My decisions won't be wise
I don't do anything for now
New thought's coming; you know how?
It will be brought to me
By this super Energy

Three popsicles, three popsicles
All you need to know
I'm living from the inside out
I'm going with the flow

And should you have a foul mood
Your thinking won't be any good
I don't believe a word you say
We'll just talk some other day
Keep it simple, keep it light
So much better than a fight

Three popsicles, three popsicles
All you need to know
I'm living from the inside out
I'm going with the flohohohooow!"

With a prolonged note, Izzy concludes her song.
Then she just improvises and plays whatever

occurs to her: "Ladi dahlalalalalalalalalalaaaaa!" After the last chord she remains silent.

There's a loud applause. Izzy looks up, startled. Mom and Dad are in the living room. Izzy hasn't heard them come in at all. "What a beautiful song!" Mom says. "Where did you get that from?" "And very well played too," Dad adds. "The vacuum cleaner sang it," Izzy replies. "And the playing went automatically." They all laugh. "I'll call it The Three Popsicles Song," Izzy beams. "I think it's going to be a number one hit," Mom says.

And what about Izzy? She's not thinking anything. She's just happy. From the inside out.